Cathy Cassidy

The Chocolate Box GIRLS

Marshmallow Skye

PUFFIN

PUFFIN BOOKS

Published by the Penguin Group
Penguin Books Ltd, 80 Strand, London WC2R ORL, England
Penguin Group (USA) Inc., 375 Hudson Street, New York, New York 10014, USA
Penguin Group (Canada), 90 Eglinton Avenue East, Suite 700, Toronto, Ontario, Canada M4P 2Y3
(a division of Pearson Penguin Canada Inc.)
Penguin Ireland, 25 St Stephen's Green, Dublin 2, Ireland (a division of Penguin Books Ltd)
Penguin Group (Australia), 707 Collins Street, Melbourne, Victoria 3008, Australia
(a division of Pearson Australia Group Pty Ltd)
Penguin Books India Pvt Ltd, 11 Community Centre, Panchsheel Park, New Delhi – 110 017, India
Penguin Group (NZ), 67 Apollo Drive, Rosedale, Auckland 0632, New Zealand
(a division of Pearson New Zealand Ltd)
Penguin Books (South Africa) (Pty) Ltd, Block D, Rosebank Office Park, 181 Jan Smuts Avenue,
Parktown North, Gauteng 2193, South Africa

Penguin Books Ltd, Registered Offices: 80 Strand, London WC2R ORL, England

puffinbooks.com

First published 2011
This edition published 2012
011

Text copyright © Cathy Cassidy, 2011
Illustrations copyright © Puffin Books, 2011
Illustrations by Julie Ingham, 2011

Set in Baskerville by Palimpsest Book Production, Falkirk, Stirlingshire
Printed in Great Britain by Clays Ltd, St Ives plc

British Library Cataloguing in Publication Data
A CIP catalogue record for this book is available from the British Library

ISBN: 978-0-141-32524-8

www.greenpenguin.co.uk

Thanks . . .

To Liam, Cal and Caitlin for being there for me, always . . . and to Mum, Joan, Andy, Lori and all my fab family. Thanks to Sheena, Helen, Fiona, Mary-Jane, Maggi, Lal and Jessie for the ongoing support, cake, party nights and hugs.

Thanks to my fab PA, Catriona, to Martyn for all the maths, and Darley and the team for being all-round fab. Huge thanks to Amanda for being the best editor ever, and to Sara and Julie for the gorgeous artwork. Thanks also to Adele, Emily, Tania, Sarah, Kirsten, Jennie, Jayde, Julia, Hannah, Rachel and all the lovely Puffins. Thanks to Rosie Fiore for being a lifesaver.

Lastly, a big thank you to Shannon for the flying rucksack story, and to all my brilliant readers . . . you really are the best!

I don't believe in ghosts.

I do believe in creaky floorboards and sudden cool draughts and eerie howling sounds when the wind whistles through the eaves, because when you live in a big, old house like Tanglewood, those things are part of the deal.

I have always lived at Tanglewood. Mum and Dad came to live here back when my big sister, Honey, was just a baby, because Grandad died very young and Grandma Kate got married again, to a Frenchman called Jules. They wanted to live in France, but Grandma Kate didn't want to sell the family house, so she gave it to us. Tanglewood is a big Victorian house just a stone's throw from the beach, and to me it is a little slice of heaven.

Some people think it's a bit spooky – and I guess I can

see why. The house actually looks like it could be haunted. Ivy clings to the soft red brick and the windows are tall and arched and criss-crossed with lead, the kind of windows where you might expect to see a face watching you: a pale, sad-eyed shadow from the past. The sort of thing you read about in books – stories where the clock strikes twelve and you wake up to mystery and intrigue and people in rustling dresses who walk right through you as if you're not there at all.

I used to wish for something like that to happen to me. I wanted to step into the past, see it for myself. I've grown up listening to ghost stories, spent summers with my sisters hunting for spooky visions and ghostly apparitions . . . but I have never seen a single one.

The only ghosts I believe in now are the Halloween variety, small and sticky-faced and dressed in white sheeting, clutching a plastic bag full of toffee apples and penny chews.

'Skye! Summer!' my sister Coco yells, sticking her head round the door. 'Aren't you two ready yet? Cherry's downstairs waiting and I've been ready for ages too, and if we don't get a move on we'll miss the party! Hurry *up*!'

❀❀❀❀❀❀❀❀❀❀❀❀❀❀❀❀❀❀❀❀❀❀❀

'Relax,' Summer says, scooshing her perfect hair with a blast of lacquer. 'We've got tons of time, Coco. It doesn't start until seven! Go duck for apples or something!'

'Skye, tell her!' my little sister wails. 'Make her hurry up!'

It is hard to take Coco seriously, though, because she has painted her face green, blacked out some of her teeth and spiked up her hair with neon gel. She is wearing a tweedy old jacket that belongs to Mum's boyfriend, Paddy, and I think she is supposed to be Frankenstein's Monster.

'Ten minutes,' I promise. 'We'll be down soon!'

Coco rolls her eyes and stomps off down the stairs.

Summer laughs. 'She is sooo impatient!'

'Just excited,' I tell my twin. 'We used to be like that, remember?'

'We're still like that, Skye,' Summer says, smoothing down her raggedy white dress. 'Just don't tell Coco! I love Halloween, don't you? It's so cool . . . like being a kid again!'

I smile. 'I know, right?'

And Summer does know, of course . . . she knows me better than anyone else in the world. She knows how I feel

❁❁❁❁❁❁❁❁❁❁❁❁❁❁❁❁❁❁❁

about a whole bunch of things, because most of the time she feels the same.

And dressing up . . . well, that's one thing we both love.

I lean in towards the mirror, pick up a brush. I am not as good with hair and make-up as my twin, but I love the magic, the moment when you glance up and see, just for a split second, a whole different person.

The girl in the mirror is pale and ghostly, a shadow girl. There are ink-dark smudges beneath her wide blue eyes, as if she hasn't slept for a week, and her hair is tangled and wild, twined with fronds of ivy and black velvet ribbon.

She looks like a girl from long ago, a girl with a story, a secret. She's the kind of girl who could make you believe in ghosts.

'Awesome,' I say, grinning, and the ghost girl grins too.

'You look gorgeous,' Summer says, as I turn away from the mirror. 'Think you'll hook up with some cute vampire boy at the party?'

'Vampire boys are a pain in the neck,' I say. Summer laughs, but the truth is that we are still at the stage of dreaming about boys in books, boys in movies, boys in bands.

4

Neither of us has a boyfriend. I like it that way, and I think Summer does too.

Besides, if you saw the boys at Exmoor Park Middle School, you would understand. They are childish and annoying and definitely not crush material, like Alfie Anderson, the class clown, who still thinks it's funny to flick chips around the canteen and set off stink bombs in the corridor.

Classy.

Summer is perched on the edge of her bed, stroking silver sparkles along her cheekbones, painting her lips to match. Our dresses are the same, skirts made from frayed, layered strips of net, chiffon and torn-up sheets, hastily stitched on to old white vest tops.

On Summer, this looks effortlessly beautiful. But when I look back at the mirror I can see that I was fooling myself – on me, it just looks slightly crazy and deranged. I am not a ghost girl, just a kid playing dress-up, and not quite as well as my sister.

I guess that is the story of my life.

Summer and I are identical twins. Mum actually has a scan from when she was pregnant, where the two of us are curled up together inside her, like kittens. It looks as if we

❀❀❀❀❀❀❀❀❀❀❀❀❀❀❀❀❀❀❀❀❀❀❀

are holding hands. The picture is fuzzy and grey, like a TV screen when the signal is lousy and everything looks crackly and broken up, but still, it's the most amazing image.

Summer came into the world first, a whole four minutes ahead of me, dazzling, daring, determined to shine. I followed after, pink-faced and howling.

They washed us and dried us and wrapped us in matching blankets and placed us in Mum's arms, and what was the first thing we did? You got it. We held hands.

That's the way it has always been, really. We were like two sides of the same coin, mirror-image kids, each a perfect reflection of the other.

Right from the start, we each knew what the other one was thinking. We finished each other's sentences, went everywhere together, shared hopes and dreams as well as toys and food and clothes and friends. We were each other's best friend. No – more than that. We *were* each other.

'Aren't they gorgeous?' people would say. 'Aren't they the sweetest things you ever saw in your life?'

And Summer would squeeze my hand and tilt her head to one side, and I'd do the same, and we'd laugh and run away from the adults, back to our own little world.

❀❀❀❀❀❀❀❀❀❀❀❀❀❀❀❀❀❀❀❀❀❀

For the longest time, I didn't know just where Summer ended and I began. I looked at her to know what I was feeling, and if she was smiling, I smiled too. If she was crying, I'd wipe away her tears and put my arms around her, and wait for the ache inside to fade.

It sounds cheesy, but if she was hurting, I hurt too.

I thought it would be that way forever, but that's not the way it's working out.

We both went to ballet class back then – we were ballet crazy. We had pink ballet bags with little pink ballet pumps and pink scrunchies, books full of ballet stories, and a whole box at home filled with tutus and fairy wings and wands. Looking back, I think I always liked the dressing up bit more than the actual dancing, but it took me a while to see that I was only crazy about ballet because Summer was. I saw her passion for dance, and I thought I felt it too . . . but really I was just a mirror girl, reflecting my twin.

I started to get fed up with ballet exams where Summer won distinctions and I struggled to scrape a pass; fed up with dance shows where Summer had a leading role while

7

I was hidden away at the back of the chorus. She had a talent for dance, I didn't . . . and bit by bit, it was chipping away at my confidence. After one of these shows where everyone came up and told Summer how brilliant she was, I finally found the courage to admit that I didn't want to go to ballet any more. It was the year that Dad moved out and everything was changing. Changing one more thing didn't seem like such a big deal, to me at least.

Summer didn't get it, though. 'You can't stop, Skye!' she argued. 'It's because you're upset about Dad leaving, isn't it? You love ballet!'

'No,' I told her. 'And this has nothing to do with Dad. *You* love ballet, Summer. Not *me*.'

Summer looked at me with her face all crumpled and confused, as if she didn't understand the whole idea of *you* and *me*. Well, I was just getting to grips with it myself. Up until then, it had always been *us*.

Lately, I have been wondering if that whole dancing thing might just have been the start of it. Sometimes, when you change one thing, the whole pattern falls apart, shattered, like the little pieces in a kaleidoscope. I guess I shook things

❀❀❀❀❀❀❀❀❀❀❀❀❀❀❀❀❀❀❀❀❀

up between my twin and me, and three years on we are still waiting for the dust to settle.

I turn back to the mirror, and for a moment I see the ghost girl again, all wild hair and sad, haunted eyes, lips parted as though she is trying to tell me something.

Then she is gone.

2

The kitchen smells of toffee and chocolate. Mum is at the Aga, skewering apples and dipping them into a pan of golden melted toffee for us to take down to the party, and Paddy has brought a batch of toffee-apple truffle mix over from the workshop for us to try.

'Just taste,' he says. 'This could be the one, the flavour that catapults us to fame and fortune . . .'

Paddy and his daughter Cherry moved in with us in the summer, and it feels as if they belong. They are like a couple of jigsaw pieces we didn't even know were missing. There is still a jagged hole where Dad used to be, but we are getting better at stepping round it, and having Paddy and Cherry here somehow helps. Cherry is cool and kind and funny, like a cross between a sister and a friend. Paddy laughs a lot and plays the violin, and he has turned the old stables into a workshop for the business he and Mum have launched, The Chocolate Box. The smell of melted chocolate wraps itself round the house these days, and there is no way that could ever be a bad thing.

Mum and Paddy are getting married in June, so we'll be a proper family then. Cherry and Paddy make everything better.

Well, almost everything.

We crowd round to taste the mixture: two ghost girls, a grinning Frankenstein (Coco) and a witch (Cherry). The truffle mix tastes exactly like Halloween, dark and sweet and autumnal.

Cherry's boyfriend Shay Fletcher is here too, wearing a werewolf mask with a shock of grey fur attached, pretending to bite Fred, the dog. I'm kind of surprised to see him. He used to go out with my big sister Honey, but when Paddy and Cherry moved in, everything changed and Shay ended up with Cherry.

See? Boys mess everything up, even nice ones like Shay. If he hadn't fallen for Cherry, then maybe Honey and Cherry would have had half a chance of getting along.

❀❀❀❀❀❀❀❀❀❀❀❀❀❀❀❀❀❀❀❀❀❀

Maybe. Things would definitely be easier around here if they did.

When Cherry and Shay got together, Honey was not amused. She cried and yelled and locked herself in her room for days on end, and when she came out again she had chopped off her beautiful, waist-length blonde hair with the kitchen scissors, so that it stuck up in little tufts from her head. Most girls would have looked like a scarecrow with a DIY haircut like that, but Honey always manages to look model-girl cool, with fierce, faraway eyes and lips that are in constant pout-mode. I said that Paddy and Cherry make everything better, but my sister Honey would not agree.

Shay has been steering clear of the house lately, for obvious reasons. I would not want to be in his shoes, or Cherry's, if Honey catches them together.

'I'm guessing Honey is out tonight?' Summer asks, reading my thoughts.

'I think so,' Cherry says, adjusting her witch outfit nervously. 'She said the Halloween party would be lame, that she had something way better to do . . .'

'Whatever,' Shay shrugs, pushing back the werewolf mask. His sandy hair is sticking up, his ocean-coloured eyes laughing. 'We have to face her some time. It's been two months now – it's time to let go, move on.'

'Ri-ight,' I say.

I am not sure that Honey would want to let go or move on if she saw Shay Fletcher in our kitchen right now. I think she might want to grab him round the neck and hang on very hard indeed, until he keels right over and dies. After that, she might 'move on' to Cherry.

I don't say any of this out loud.

'Hey,' I say instead, trying to round everybody up. 'We have a party to go to, and we're meeting Millie and Tia at the hall. Don't want to keep them waiting!'

'Exactly,' Coco says. 'Come on, you lot!'

Everyone is talking and laughing and putting on jackets, but we are not fast enough. Honey appears in the doorway, and the laughter dies. The atmosphere is so frosty you'd need an ice pick to even dent it. I can practically see the icicles forming all around me.

She is dressed as a vampire girl, in a cute crimson mini-dress with her face and neck powdered pale. Two red puncture marks are painted on at the base of her neck, just above her collarbone.

❀❀❀❀❀❀❀❀❀❀❀❀❀❀❀❀❀❀❀❀❀❀

The costume's pretty good – because my sister is not as sweet as she looks. Ever since Dad left she has swung between tears and tantrums and just enough little-girl charm to keep the rest of us wound round her little finger. Then Shay ditched her, and Dad had a promotion to open an overseas branch of the firm he works for, and announced he was going to live in Australia. He left a couple of weeks ago.

It's not as if Dad was very good at birthdays or Christmas or weekend visits – he wasn't. But there is only one thing worse than having a hopeless dad, and that's having a hope-less dad on the other side of the world. Personally, I cannot quite forgive him.

And, what with the Shay-thing and Dad moving abroad, Honey has dropped any pretence at charm. These days she is like a whirlwind of don't-care, in-your-face attitude.

Honey glances at Shay and I can see him shrink away under her gaze.

'What do you think you're doing here, loser?' she asks icily.

Mum turns round sharply from the Aga. 'Honey!' she says. 'Whatever you might think of Shay, that's no way to talk to a guest!'

Honey doesn't seem to hear. The rest of us stand there awkwardly.

'It's OK, Charlotte,' Shay says to Mum. 'I'm sorry. Looks like I misjudged things. I thought it was time we buried the hatchet . . .'

Honey laughs, and I am pretty sure that if there was a hatchet anywhere around right now, she would know exactly where to bury it.

'I didn't think you were going to this party, Honey!' Mum says, trying to steer the conversation on to safer ground.

'As if,' Honey snarls. 'I'm going into town with Alex.'

'Alex?' Mum echoes, but Honey ignores the question.

She glances at Cherry, whose witch costume is a black T-shirt, miniskirt and stripy tights, with toy spiders in her hair and a broomstick she made herself from birch twigs tied on to a twisty branch.

Honey raises an eyebrow.

'Aren't you supposed to dress up?' she says nastily, and Cherry's cheeks flood with pink.

Then there's the roar of a motorbike on the gravel outside and my big sister runs out into the darkness.

'Hang on a minute!' Paddy calls after her, but she slams

❀❀❀❀❀❀❀❀❀❀❀❀❀❀❀❀❀❀❀❀❀

the door in his face. We hear the motorbike roar away, and then silence.

'Who is this Alex boy?' Mum asks. 'How old is he, anyway?'

'Old enough to have a motorbike,' Paddy frowns.

'Honey's fourteen!' Mum wails. 'Just a child! And we've let her ride off into the night on a motorbike, with a boy we've never met!'

'You couldn't have stopped her, Mum,' I say.

That's Honey . . . you can't stop her. She used to be the coolest sister in the world, but now she is way out of reach, an alien creature in too much black mascara and lipgloss, with a never-ending line-up of scary boyfriends. She's off the rails – and there's nothing at all we can do about it.

3

The evening goes downhill from there.

Millie and Tia are waiting for us outside the hall. We've been best friends since we were little kids . . . Tia and Summer, and Millie and me. One look at their faces tells me that the party, as Honey predicted, is lame. There are lots of little kids ducking for apples and mums sipping blood-red punch that is really just cranberry juice. There are biscuits with green icing shaped like severed fingers and the tray of toffee apples we carried down from Mum. There are cool pumpkin lanterns that flicker and glint, but still, we are the oldest kids there by a mile. We slope off early to trick-or-treat around the village, and manage to collect a plastic cauldron full of toffee and peanuts and weird gummy sweets that look like eyeballs.

Maybe I am getting too old for Halloween after all, because I am sick of cheesy, spooky jokes and I have eaten so many sweets I think my teeth might dissolve. 'This is no fun,' Summer declares, reading my mind. 'Let's go home.'

'It's only half eight!' Coco argues. 'And it's Halloween!'

'We can't go home yet,' Millie groans.

'Why don't you all come back to the caravan?' Cherry suggests. 'Paddy said he'd light the stove, so it should be warm, and I have Irn-Bru . . . we could tell ghost stories!'

Coco's eyes light up. 'Oh, let's! That'd be cool!'

'Sounds like a plan,' I say.

We are walking up past the church when Cherry stops and frowns, looking around anxiously. 'Did you hear something?' she asks. 'Like . . . well, ghostly footsteps?'

'Ghosts don't have footsteps!' Coco says. 'They just glide right through you, like a cold finger sliding down your spine!'

'There's nothing there, Cherry,' Shay promises.

We move on, but seconds later a tall, grey-skinned zombie, trailing lengths of bloodstained bandages, leaps out from behind a gravestone, wild-eyed and moaning, right in front of us.

18

I take a closer look and sigh, exasperated. Alfie Anderson is possibly the most annoying boy at Exmoor Park Middle School, and practical jokes are his speciality. *Bad* practical jokes. I have known him since the first day of primary school, and he has not improved with age.

'Alfie, what are you playing at?' Summer asks. 'You just about gave me heart failure. It's OK, Cherry – he's harmless. Meet the village nutter.'

'Hey,' Alfie says, raising an eyebrow. 'It was just a joke.'

'Jokes are supposed to be funny,' Summer says. She hooks an arm into Cherry's and marches away along the lane with Millie, Tia, Shay and Coco following. I am left with Alfie, his shoulders drooping.

'Where are you all going?' he asks. 'What about the party?'

'We've been, and it wasn't very good. We're heading home to tell ghost stories,' I say, and Alfie's face lights up.

'I know lots of those! Really bloodthirsty ones. Can I come?'

I hesitate. Summer finds Alfie deeply annoying, and so do I except in very small doses, but it seems really mean to say no.

'Er . . . well . . .'

But Alfie is striding on ahead. 'I love ghost stories. Ghouls, zombies, axe-wielding maniacs . . . awesome stuff.'

I roll my eyes and head off after Alfie and the others, out of the village and along the quiet lane that leads up to Tanglewood House. Ancient trees dip down, whispering, over the hedgerows and a barn owl hoots eerily and swoops down low above us with a flash of white wings.

'A ghost!' Coco yelps, thrilled.

'An owl,' I say. 'There's no such thing as ghosts, you know that!'

'There might be,' she argues. 'It's Halloween! I read about it – it's the one night of the year when the veil between the world of the living and the dead lifts a little –'

'Woo-hoo-hoo!' Alfie Anderson yells. And he clowns around all the way up the lane, across the gravel drive at Tanglewood and down to the gypsy caravan.

When Cherry first arrived, she and Honey had to share a room – that lasted about five minutes because Honey was weird about Cherry from the start, even before the whole Shay-disaster. Cherry has been camped out in the caravan ever since. It's beautiful, a real traveller wagon, carefully restored and parked under the trees. Even so, Cherry would rather be in the house with us, I think. And although there are no spare rooms in the main bit of the house, because Tanglewood House is a B&B, Paddy has promised to clear out the attic so that Cherry can have a little room of her own by Christmas.

We pile into the caravan, shoe-horning ourselves in, the little woodburner roaring. It might be a world record for the most people to fit inside a gypsy caravan, but it's fun. Cherry pours Irn-Bru into tin mugs and we pass round the trick-or-treat sweets just in case there is any danger of our blood sugar levels dipping down towards normal.

The ghost stories begin. Alfie tells an especially gruesome one about a headless horseman, Shay tells us about the shipwrecked smugglers who supposedly haunt the coast, and Cherry shares a beautiful Japanese tale that may or may not be based on her mum, who died when she was a toddler.

'Are there any stories about Tanglewood?' Shay wants to know.

'Sure,' Summer says. 'Grandma Kate used to tell us lots of stories about the place . . .'

'Stories?' Cherry prompts.

'This house has been in the family for years,' I say. 'And Grandma Kate knew all the stories. One of them was kind of spooky . . .'

'Oh, about Clara?' Coco exclaims. 'I love that one. It's so, so sad!'

Alfie scrunches up his face. 'Can't we have gory, instead?'

'Quiet, Alfie,' Summer huffs. 'It's a love story, about a girl who fell for the wrong boy . . .'

Cherry glances at Shay, and I remember that she has fallen for the 'wrong' boy too, at least as far as Honey is concerned.

'Clara Travers lived here, at Tanglewood, back in the 1920s,' Summer begins. 'She was a relative of Grandma Kate's from way back. She was seventeen, and engaged to be married to an older man, with a big house in London . . .'

I pick up the story where Summer leaves off. 'Clara's fiancé was rich, and her parents thought the match was a good one,' I continue. 'But she didn't love him. She fell for a gypsy boy, one of the Romany travellers who sometimes camped in the woods nearby. They planned to run away together, but Clara's parents found out. Her father was furious . . . He chased the travellers away and told them never to return.'

Cherry bites her lip. 'That's sooo sad!'

'That's not the end,' Coco says, wide-eyed. 'Tell her, Skye!'

I take a deep breath. 'When Clara saw that the travellers had gone, she was heartbroken,' I say. 'The day before she was due to marry her fiancé, she left her clothes folded in a little pile on the beach and swam out into the ocean. She was never seen again.'

'Her ghost is supposed to wander the woods,' Coco declares. 'Crying and looking for her lost love . . . that's what Grandma Kate used to say!'

'Oh!' Millie says. 'Spooky!'

'It's a sad story,' I shrug. 'But there is no ghost, obviously . . . we've been looking for years, and we've never seen a single thing.'

'That doesn't mean anything, though,' Coco says. 'She could be here right now, listening . . .'

A silence falls, and into the silence comes a rustling of leaves overhead and the soft hooting of the barn owl. It's probably a sugar rush from way too many sweets, but my heart begins to race.

'Boo!' Alfie yells, and the moment is lost. Everyone is

23

talking again, too fast, too loud. Tia texts her mum to arrange a lift home for her and Millie, and when the car arrives Shay and Alfie grab a lift too. The rest of us head back up to the house, bursting into the warm, bright kitchen in a muddle of laughter and chat.

Paddy and Mum look up at us, startled, their faces smudged with dust. A huddle of cardboard boxes sit in the corner of the kitchen, piled up with junk and stuff I've never seen before. A birdcage made of powder-blue wire arranged in ornate twists perches on top of one box, and up on the kitchen table is an old pine trunk, the curving lid pulled back to reveal layers of tissue paper and fabric and what might be a battered leather violin case.

'What is all this?' I ask. My heart is racing again, my mouth dry.

Paddy flicks a cobweb from his hair. 'We thought we'd make a start on clearing that attic space for Cherry's bedroom,' he explains. 'We've filled the van with stuff for the tip and dragged a load of boxes out to the workshop to be sorted, but right in the far corner we found this trunk . . .'

The kitchen is suddenly silent as two ghost girls, a witch and a green-faced monster crowd round to look. I reach out to touch the crumpled tissue paper, and my fingertips brush soft velvet, crisp cotton lace.

'This stuff looks really old!' I whisper.

Mum picks up a slim bundle of letters, all tied up together with ribbon, from the top of the trunk.

'It is old,' she says. 'Girls, I don't suppose you remember that old story your gran used to tell? A sad story, about a girl called Clara Travers? As far as we can see from the letters, these were Clara's things . . .'

A shiver runs down my spine.

Ten minutes ago we were huddled in the caravan telling long-ago ghost stories of a girl called Clara. Now all her things are right here, spread out before us in the warm glow of the kitchen. Letters, violins, velvet – these are echoes of a past that we can only guess at, of a future that ended abruptly in the cold, dark ocean.

Forget Alfie Anderson's graveyard prank – this is easily the spookiest thing that has happened all night.

4

The next day, Summer has a ballet class after school and Coco, Cherry and I are in the kitchen, ploughing through homework while Mum makes marshmallow cupcakes. Marshmallow has always been my favourite taste in the world, although Summer has never been keen.

'It's so boring,' she used to say, wrinkling up her nose. 'So plain. Sweet but nothingy.'

I've always had this horrible feeling that she thinks I'm boring and plain and nothingy too, for liking it.

But to me marshmallow isn't boring at all. It is soft and sweet and fluffy, a little piece of heaven.

I spot the old pine trunk, still sitting in a corner, and like last night, the tiniest shiver runs down my spine. I'm not sure whether it comes from fear or excitement.

❀ ❀ ❀ ❀ ❀ ❀ ❀ ❀ ❀ ❀ ❀ ❀ ❀ ❀ ❀ ❀ ❀

'Mum?' I ask, as she sets the cupcakes on a rack to cool, 'I was wondering . . . what are you actually going to do with the trunk from the attic?'

Mum frowns. 'Well, I don't know . . . all that stuff is probably worth quite a bit to an antiques dealer. And we could really use the money right now. It'll be Christmas in a couple of months.'

'No!' I protest. 'Don't sell them!'

I don't know why, but the thought of Clara's things being sold feels wrong.

Mum frowns. 'But we haven't got anywhere to put them – Paddy's about to clear out the attic, so we'd just end up having to store them in the workshop . . . Although Summer did take the blue birdcage at breakfast time – said she was going to put a plant in it. Would any of the rest of you like something from the trunk?'

'Me!' Coco pipes up. 'The violin! I have always wanted one, and Paddy said he'd teach me if I had something to practise on.'

'Is that a good idea?' Mum asks. 'Coco, you are totally gorgeous and wonderful and talented, but I am not certain that music is your strong point! Remember the time you tried to learn the recorder for that Christmas carol concert back in Year Three?'

Coco may not, but I do. She drove us all crazy, until one day the recorder went mysteriously missing and was never seen again.

'Shame,' Honey had said at the time, ruffling Coco's hair. 'It seems to have vanished into thin air!'

I think it may actually have vanished into the dustbin, with a little help from Honey, but all of us breathed a huge sigh of relief. Coco had to play the cowbells instead, and even then she couldn't keep to the beat.

'This will be different,' Coco insists now. 'Paddy will teach me. Properly. Please?'

'I suppose,' Mum says doubtfully, licking a curl of vanilla frosting from her fingertip and dotting golden-brown toasted mini marshmallows across the freshly iced cakes. Coco dives into the trunk and rescues the battered leather case, opening it up to reveal a glossy golden violin. She lifts it to her shoulder and saws the bow across it, and a sound like several cats being strangled fills the kitchen.

'Ouch,' Coco says. 'It's not as easy as it looks . . .'

Mum offers the plate of still-warm cupcakes around,

28

and I take one eagerly, biting into melting marshmallow sprinkles.

'What about you, Cherry? Is there anything you'd like from the trunk?'

'Not really,' Cherry says. 'It's awesome, but . . . well, it's just a bit too spooky for me.'

'OK, Skye, so if you don't want me to sell it, do you want anything from the trunk? The dresses, maybe?'

I blink. 'No way . . . those dresses . . . could I really have them?'

'Why not?' Mum says. 'You love vintage clothes, don't you? I think Clara would have wanted you to have them.'

Half an hour later, the pine trunk is sitting next to my bed in the room Summer and I share. I lift the lid and push aside the crumpled tissue paper. For a moment I breathe in the faintest scent of marshmallow, a heady mixture of warm vanilla and sugar. Then it's gone, replaced by the whiff of dust and age and sadness. Was it the aroma of Mum's cupcakes, drifting up from the kitchen, or the remnants of some long-ago perfume? Although I'm not sure the scent would last all that time. It's probably just my imagination.

Last night, the whole idea of Clara's trunk was so spooky

I didn't look too carefully at what was inside . . . but it's like treasure.

The trunk is filled with jewel-bright velvet shift dresses and petticoats made of white cotton lace. There are crinkled leather shoes with little heels, straw hats and cloche hats, and white gloves of soft suede. There is a feathered head-band and silver bracelets tarnished dark with age, a beaded clutch bag, and folded carefully, right at the bottom, a soft woollen coat the colour of emeralds, lined with green satin.

I slip the coat on, button it up, let the skirt spin out around me. This coat is soft and warm and barely worn at all, a million times better than my usual jumble sale finds. Every-thing in the trunk is perfect, as though it were put away just yesterday and not ninety years ago.

I try on the white cotton petticoats, the velvet shift dresses, one at a time . . . midnight blue, moss green, crimson. Clara Travers must have been small and slender because the clothes seem to fit. I don't look like a child wearing adult clothes, not at all. A while ago I read a book about the 1920s, all jazz records and flapper girls. I pull on a cloche hat, peer out from under the rim, grinning, looking in the mirror for traces of a flapper girl from long ago.

❀❀❀❀❀❀❀❀❀❀❀❀❀❀❀❀❀❀❀❀❀❀❀

Judging by the cool clothes, I am pretty certain that Clara Travers liked to dance, that she listened to jazz music and learned the Charleston and had a dozen young men queuing up to dance with her in her bright flapper dresses and feathered headband. She was a cool girl, a party girl, I know it. Wearing these clothes, I suddenly feel a bit that way too . . . brave, beautiful, grown-up.

Then I remember Grandma Kate's story – that Clara was engaged to be married to a man much older than herself, and my smile fades.

Who was Clara Travers? I wonder to myself. *A rich girl with a trunkful of velvet dresses, an armful of bangles, a head filled with dreams?* She was seventeen, just three years older than Honey is now. That seems way too young to be tied down to a man she didn't love. I try to imagine Honey being paired off with some old bloke of thirty or forty, and shudder. It must have felt like the end of everything.

Was there ever a romance, or was it just an alliance made for money, security, status? Did Clara's parents arrange it all? And how did a girl like Clara fall in love with a gypsy, so much in love she couldn't see a future without him?

❁❁❁❁❁❁❁❁❁❁❁❁❁❁❁❁❁❁❁❁❁❁

The bedroom door swings open and Summer comes in, her hair still pinned up from dance class, her ballet bag swinging.

'Mum says tea's ready in ten minutes,' she says, then stops short as she sees me properly.

Suddenly, I don't feel like a beautiful 1920s girl any more, just a little kid caught doing something she shouldn't.

'What is all that, Skye?' she asks. 'Why are you wearing those creepy old clothes?'

Just as it did earlier when Mum mentioned the possibility of selling Clara's things, a strong feeling surfaces inside me.

'They're not creepy, just old,' I say, and my eyes light on the old powder-blue birdcage with the twisty wire bars that now sits in the corner behind Summer's bed. 'Like your birdcage. Vintage chic, right?'

'It's different,' Summer insists. 'The birdcage is one thing, but don't you think it's a bit weird, actually wearing Clara's things? I mean . . . she's dead. It's just too spooky.'

I laugh. 'I love vintage clothes. I wear old stuff all the time . . .'

Summer raises an eyebrow. 'That's different. Clara

32

Travers killed herself,' she huffs. 'Please, Skye, take her things off. I don't like it.'

I pull off the cloche hat, and as I do I catch a glimpse of my reflection. For a moment I look defiant, determined – not like me at all. I blink, and the illusion is gone. The mirror just shows a smiley girl with wavy blonde hair, wearing a dress from long ago.

I pull the crimson flapper dress over my head and fold it carefully back into the trunk, but I leave the white cotton petticoat, the bracelets. I pull on a jumper, twirl round in front of the mirror.

It looks good, but Summer still seems troubled.

'What?' I say to her, trying to laugh it off. 'You think Clara's going to haunt me? Come on! I mean . . . seriously?'

'No, of course not,' Summer says. 'But . . . well, maybe the stories are right, and her spirit does roam around Tangle-wood? Looking for her lost love?' I mean, don't you think it was strange that last night we'd just been talking about Clara Travers, and then a few minutes later we went inside and all her things had turned up after almost a hundred years of being lost? On Halloween, as well!'

'Hey, hey,' I whisper. 'That stuff was never lost, it was in the attic the whole time. It's just coincidence that Paddy started to clear the attic on Halloween. It doesn't *mean* anything, Summer!'

Summer sighs. 'I don't know. I don't like it . . .'

I try to shrug away her concern. There's no way that anything genuinely spooky is going on.

Like I said, I don't believe in ghosts . . .

5

I step outside, closing the door behind me softly, and the grass beneath my feet is studded with daisies and the air smells marshmallow sweet. I am wearing a blue velvet dress and little shoes with a button strap, and my wrists jangle with silver bracelets – shiny bright, like new.

I slip out through the little picket gate with the mallow flowers arched on either side, and run into the woods, with the sun shining down through a canopy of green.

I walk down through the trees, my heart beating fast, a soft flutter of excitement bubbling up inside. And then I smell woodsmoke, and looking down through the branches of the twisty hazel trees I can see four bow-top gypsy wagons in the clearing below.

A woodfire smoulders nearby, a blackened kettle hanging above it, and half a dozen horses, big and patterned with variations of black and white, are grazing nearby. Two small girls in raggedy dresses play *a hiding game among the trees, and a couple of dark-haired men are mending pots and pans beside the fire.*

There's the sound of twigs breaking softly behind me, and a skinny, dishevelled dog that looks like a tawny-coloured toilet brush rushes up and nudges my hand. I stroke the dog and scratch its ears, and turn round slowly. Suddenly, my heart does a backflip inside my chest and my cheeks flush.

The boy walking towards me through the trees is a stranger, but it feels like I have known him forever. He is tall and tanned, with dark hair that flops down across his face and eyes so blue they take my breath away. His clothes are strange, old-fashioned, a white shirt with no collar and the sleeves rolled up, a threadbare waistcoat and cord trousers the colour of bracken. At his neck is a red scarf, knotted carelessly.

Just then, a bird flies up from a nearby branch, a flash of red and brown, a flurry of wings.

Finch, *I think.* The boy's name is Finch.

'Hey,' he says, and his face breaks into a grin. His hand reaches out to catch mine, holding tight.

I sit up, pushing the hair back from my face, my heart racing. I wonder where I am for a moment, but in the half-light of dawn I can see I'm in the room I share with my twin. I

❀❀❀❀❀❀❀❀❀❀❀❀❀❀❀❀❀❀❀❀❀❀

remember trying on Clara's clothes last night, before supper, then squabbling with Summer about it. I remember Summer, Cherry and Coco choosing a DVD and curling up on the sofas to watch, but I was tired and sloped off to my room, flaking out early.

'That,' I say out loud, 'was the weirdest dream ever.'

'Huh?' Summer murmurs from under her duvet. 'What dream?'

'It seemed so real,' I frown. 'Like it was actually happening. But I wasn't really me. Or if I was, then everything else was just kind of muddled and wrong . . . I don't know. Weird.'

Summer doesn't reply, but she blinks at me with sleepy, troubled eyes, her brows slanting into a frown.

That's when I realize I am still wearing the white cotton petticoat that once belonged to Clara Travers . . .

6

I don't say any more to Summer about my dream, although I'm still thinking about it all the way to school. First period is history. Mr Wolfe is new at Exmoor Park Middle School, and everyone thinks he is wired to the moon. He wears tweed jackets with elbow patches and corduroy trousers in beige or mustard yellow, and he always smells faintly of toast. He looks like he might be better suited to a career at Hogwarts, or perhaps as an extra in a horror movie featuring werewolves. No wonder Alfie Anderson likes to tease him.

I think history is cool. It's all about stories, about how the past shapes the present and the future, and I've loved it ever since I can remember. Back in Year Four I got a gold star for my Egyptian project, which involved trying to mummify a Barbie doll with lengths of toilet roll in front of the entire class. 'Awesome, Skye,' Alfie said. I think he liked the bit where I told the class how those ancient Egyptians used to remove the mummy's brains by dragging them out through the nostrils with a hook. Boys are kind of blood-thirsty for stories like that.

I think I prefer the Clara Travers kind of history – doomed love stories and amazing clothes. But even though I love history, I am not at all sure about Mr Wolfe. I can't help feeling a little bit sorry for him, though.

Today he is late coming to class, and Alfie has set up a practical joke. As the new history teacher walks into the room, a wastepaper basket balanced on top of the slightly open door topples down on him, showering him with scrunched-up paper.

He peers at us through his horn-rimmed glasses. 'Amusing,' he says. 'Do you know something, class? History is full of unpredictable events, but we can *learn* from them. They teach us to expect the unexpected –'

Mr Wolfe whips the chair out from under his desk suddenly, as if expecting to see a Whoopee cushion or a drawing pin Blu-tacked to the seat. Nothing. He checks under the table, sifts through the papers on his desk and squints at the whiteboard as if checking for traps.

'See?' he proclaims. 'History teaches us to be prepared!'

Not quite prepared enough, alas. Mr Wolfe is forgetting one very important lesson – history repeats itself.

I cannot bear to watch.

'Sir!' I say, waving my hand in the air, but Mr Wolfe just smiles and tells me to wait a moment.

He steps into the stock cupboard to fetch our textbooks, and that's when Alfie Anderson's rucksack, balanced all that time on the top of the stock-cupboard door, crashes down on top of him, knocking his glasses to the floor.

The whole class just about fall off their chairs laughing.

'History didn't teach you to expect that, Sir,' Alfie snorts.

Mr Wolfe turns a strange shade of crimson. He picks up the rucksack, which is extra heavy because Alfie has stuffed it with history textbooks to give it more oomph. His hands shake a little as he does this, and so does his voice.

'Alfie Anderson, is this your rucksack?' he asks.

'Yes, Sir!' Alfie says. 'I wonder how it got over there?'

I think what happens next is partly Alfie's fault, for push-

❀❀❀❀❀❀❀❀❀❀❀❀❀❀❀❀❀❀❀❀❀

ing Mr Wolfe too far. It is also partly Mr Wolfe's fault for losing his temper and not pausing to pick up his glasses from the floor. You could even say a part of the blame rests with Mr King, the head teacher, for being in the wrong place at the wrong time.

That is how history works, though. It is all about cause and effect, but there is a lot of luck involved.

Mr Wolfe hurls the rucksack through the air at Alfie, and it misses completely and flies right through the window, shattering glass all over the classroom. There's a squeal of brakes from outside and an outraged yell.

'What the devil is going on up there?' a familiar voice roars.

It is very unlucky indeed that the head teacher happened to be parking his car beneath the window at that exact moment. A few of us sitting near the window watch as the rucksack bounces off the roof of Mr King's new Skoda Fabia, denting it slightly, then slides to the ground, knocking off a wing mirror on the way.

'Whoa,' Alfie says. 'Nice shot, Sir!'

But Mr Wolfe sinks down on to his chair and puts his head in his hands, and this time nobody laughs at all.

❀❀❀❀❀❀❀❀❀❀❀❀❀❀❀❀❀❀❀❀❀❀

'Alfie!' I hiss. 'What have you done?'

'What have *I* done?' Alfie echoes, all innocent. 'I didn't break the window!'

'Alfie!' I growl. 'This is not funny. He could lose his job over this! Do something, or –'

'Or you're history,' Summer says crisply, from across the aisle.

A few moments later, the classroom door bursts open and Mr King storms in, carrying the rucksack. He is purple with fury.

'Mr Wolfe!' he roars. 'What is going on? How did this happen?'

The history teacher stands up, squaring his shoulders and raking a hand through his hair, but it is Alfie who speaks.

'It was me, Sir,' he says, calmly and clearly. 'I was messing around and Mr Wolfe told me to stop, and . . . it was an accident, Sir, but I was to blame.'

He hangs his head, and for the first time in living memory, I feel the tiniest bit of sympathy for Alfie Anderson.

'My office, now, Alfie,' Mr King says. 'I will send the janitor over to clean up the broken glass. Mr Wolfe, take

❀❀❀❀❀❀❀❀❀❀❀❀❀❀❀❀❀❀❀❀❀❀

your class down to the library until this mess has been cleared up.'

The door closes, and Mr Wolfe faces the class, slightly shell-shocked.

'Is . . . is anybody hurt?' he asks.

'No, Sir.'

'That's something at least,' he says. 'Well . . . as you can see, history is happening all around us, all the time. Some events stay in our minds and memories forever, and I have a feeling that was one of them.'

'Too right,' Millie mutters, beside me.

'Sometimes, though, you don't always get the full picture,' Mr Wolfe frowns. 'History isn't always what it seems, and it's all too easy to get the wrong idea. You have to piece together the clues to make sense of it all . . .'

I blink. Suddenly, Mr Wolfe is not so much werewolf as a wise history guru whose words make me catch my breath – what he says about clues makes me think about Clara Travers. Maybe I could find out more about her, piece together her story, if I can just find some more clues. The dream is still vivid in my mind, as if I actually did slip back in time and see the world through Clara's eyes for a moment.

My heart beats hard at the thought of it. Does that make it not so much a dream, but more . . . a kind of haunting?

I frown, shaking the idea out of my head.

'I'd better set the record straight,' Mr Wolfe sighs. 'History likes a hero, but I can't let Alfie take the blame for this. Go along to the library, Year Eight. I will see the head and get this sorted out.'

So, yeah . . . history. It is never boring, or at least not for long.

7

'He's not as bad as I thought,' Summer says as we pile on to the bus for Kitnor.

'Who, Mr Wolfe?' I ask. 'Or Alfie?'

Summer rolls her eyes. 'Mr Wolfe, of course,' she says. 'There is no hope whatsoever for Alfie.'

In some ways, you cannot blame Alfie Anderson for being slightly unhinged, because he has a very strange family. His parents are ageing hippies who run the village health-food store and wander around wearing tie-dye T-shirts and smelling of patchouli oil, which is a little bit like the smell of a cat litter tray in my opinion. His two little sisters wear lots of handknitted sweaters and skirts that jingle when they walk. I guess Alfie is just trying to be different, and you can't blame him for that.

I think there might be hope for him, actually. A glimmer.

And then I change my mind, because the minute I sit down he legs it along the aisle and flops down beside me in the seat I was saving for Millie.

'Old Wolfie was a legend, back there,' he tells me. 'Mr King was about to ring my parents . . . I could have been kicked out. And then Wolfie waded in and I am off the hook, except for a week's worth of lunchtime detentions. Y'know, I think I could get to like history lessons, although I am more interested in actually *making* history than writing about it . . .'

Alfie's brown hair is gelled into three or four different directions, which makes him look a little like he has just crawled out of a wind tunnel. I don't think he is likely to be making history with his charm, good looks or personal style, at least not any time soon.

Millie gets on the bus and tries to nudge Alfie out of the way with her schoolbag, but he will not move. He seems to be settling in for the day.

'Millie, Millie,' he says, shaking his head. 'You are a lovely girl, but Skye and I would like a bit of privacy right now. We have important matters to discuss.'

'Weirdo,' my friend says, flopping down into a seat across

the aisle. The bus lurches into action, and I am stranded with the most annoying boy in the whole of Year Eight. Great.

'What are you playing at, Alfie?' I huff. 'I will not do your history homework for you, if that's what you're thinking!'

'As if!' he protests, holding his hands up in surrender. 'Although it would probably be fun for you, Skye, because you love history. You wear all that freaky vintage stuff and everything . . .'

He flicks my stripy scarf and shoots a meaningful look at my navy blazer and matching beret. OK, I admit I am the only person on the bus wearing a school blazer. I admit I found it in a jumble sale, and added in the scarf and beret because I'd seen them in an ancient kid's book about a boarding school. I admit I am probably the only kid at Exmoor Park Middle School who sometimes gets told off for actually *wearing* school uniform.

Is it my fault it's fifty years out of date? I happen to have a special interest in the history of fashion.

'So anyway,' Alfie ploughs on. 'I need some advice. It's serious.' He lowers his voice and looks around the bus, anxiously. 'I'm in love. Can you meet me in the Mad Hatter on Saturday to talk about it?'

✿✿✿✿✿✿✿✿✿✿✿✿✿✿✿✿✿✿✿✿✿✿✿

My tummy flips over . . . and not in a good way. More in a queasy, please-don't-let-this-be-happening way.

I remember Alfie jumping out on us by the graveyard at Halloween, almost as if he had been waiting for us. I remember the way he stopped clowning around and took the blame in the classroom earlier on after I glared at him. This is bad . . . very, very bad.

'No!' I squeak, horrified. 'I mean, I am very . . . um . . . flattered. Of course. But . . . I just don't feel the same. At all!'

Alfie looks confused. 'Flattered?' he echoes. 'Huh? What are you talking about?'

'You,' I say patiently. 'And . . . well, me.'

Alfie Anderson laughs so hard then I think he might do himself an injury. 'No, no, NO!' he says, once he has recovered the power of speech. 'I am not in love with *you*, Skye, obviously!'

I am torn between a deep sense of relief and feeling slightly offended that the idea of being in love with me should be quite so hysterically funny.

Alfie notices my frown.

'Not that there's any reason why someone *wouldn't* fancy

48

you,' he says quickly. 'It's just that you're a mate, y'know? Not that you are actually hideous or anything.'

'Thank you,' I say huffily. 'I think.'

'No worries,' Alfie shrugs. 'But anyway, I need some advice, and obviously, we can't talk properly here on the bus, so I thought if we met up this Saturday –'

'I'm busy,' I tell him. Which is true because we are having a beach bonfire on Saturday, and there is no way on earth I am asking Alfie along to that.

When I was little, we used to have a bonfire in the garden every fifth of November. We'd dress up warmly in woolly hats and scarves and eat sausage and mash from tin plates. We'd write our names in the air with sizzling sparklers and Dad would stress and growl as he set up flashy rockets and fireworks brought down from London.

Then Dad left, and everything changed. We started going down into Kitnor for the annual firework display instead, and it was still cool, but not as cool as the bonfire days had been.

This year, Mum and Paddy have decided to have a DIY bonfire again, but down on the beach instead of in the garden – a new tradition, a new beginning.

'So . . . Sunday?' Alfie Anderson persists.

'Homework,' I say. 'Sorry.'

'Next Saturday then?'

I sigh. Alfie is not about to give up, I can see that, and to be honest he could do with a few lessons in how to behave around girls. Around anyone, in fact.

'I'll think about it,' I say.

Without warning, Alfie Anderson flings his arms round me in a messy hug that smells of Lynx bodyspray and school stew. In case you are wondering, this is not a good combination. Over his shoulder, I can see Summer, Millie and Tia, pulling disgusted faces and pretending to make themselves sick.

'Alfie!' I yell sternly. 'Get off!'

He pulls back hastily, holding his hands up in surrender. 'OK, OK, don't get excited,' he says. 'We're just good friends, remember? My heart belongs to another.'

On reflection, I am very glad about that.

Later, when we're back at Tanglewood, Summer is practising pliés and pirouettes in the bedroom while I paint my nails with a cast-off nail varnish she's just given me – a shimmery purple shade called Misty Sunrise. It's not really my style, but I don't want to seem ungrateful.

✿✿✿✿✿✿✿✿✿✿✿✿✿✿✿✿✿✿✿✿✿✿✿✿✿

'He fancies you, y'know – Alfie Anderson,' Summer says carelessly, pointing a toe. 'Unlucky!'

I chuck my pillow at her, and she catches it neatly before it crashes into the vintage birdcage, which is now hanging from the ceiling by the window. Summer has put a little climbing plant inside, one whose leafy tendrils twine up and around the powder-blue bars as well as hanging down. It's pretty, even if it is swinging a little wildly right at this moment.

'Watch it, vandal,' Summer says, and chucks the pillow back at me.

I reach for the cotton wool and nail-varnish remover. 'You've smudged my nail varnish. Typical.'

'Not my fault you have violent tendencies,' Summer smirks. 'Better make sure your nails are perfect if you want to hook Alfie!'

'Don't be mean,' I say. 'I do not want to hook Alfie Anderson, and trust me, he does not fancy me. He was just asking my advice because he has a crush on someone else.'

'Yeah?' Summer asks. 'Believe that and you'll believe anything. Don't encourage him, Skye – boys are nothing but trouble. I am definitely sticking to ballet.'

51

'I won't encourage Alfie,' I say. 'He is the least romantic boy I have ever met.'

'Romance is trouble too,' Summer warns, resting her arm on the window sill to run through her barre work. 'It always ends in tragedy. Look at Romeo and Juliet, or Shay and Honey . . . Or Mum and Dad . . .'

I finish repainting my nails and waft them about to dry.

'Well, how about Mum and Paddy?' I argue. 'Not all love affairs are doomed. They're getting married in June!'

'There's always the odd exception,' Summer shrugs. 'Paddy's OK, I admit. But mostly, these things end in tears. Look at your creepy Clara and her gypsy boy . . .'

I think of a boy with blue eyes and a red neckerchief and tanned hands holding mine, and my heart races. I let go of the thought abruptly.

'She's not "my" Clara,' I say. 'And she's not creepy! She's . . . well, an ancestor of ours. It's family history, Summer, and it's so sad. She must have loved her gypsy boy a lot, to risk everything like that.'

'And he let her down,' Summer reminds me. 'Typical boy.'

8

Saturday feels like the first day of winter.

Summer has a ballet class and Honey is holed up in her room, but Coco, Cherry and I help Mum with the guest breakfasts and room changes, and then head down to the beach where Paddy is building a bonfire for later.

There's a raw wind blowing in from the ocean as we scour the beach for driftwood. We find weathered branches washed pale by the sea, dragging them back along the sand while Fred the dog runs circles around us, barking, his tail thrashing madly.

Paddy builds a pyramid of storm-worn wood, and Coco, Cherry and I hang lanterns from the handrail of the cliff path that leads down from the garden to the beach, so we don't trip and fall in the darkness.

❀❀❀❀❀❀❀❀❀❀❀❀❀❀❀❀❀❀❀❀❀❀

'Is Shay coming?' Coco dares to ask. 'Because that might mean Honey won't come, and Mum asked her specially, and she said she would . . .'

'I told him not to,' Cherry says. 'The last thing I want is to make Honey feel like she can't come to her own family's bonfire party.'

'She might not come anyway,' I say. 'You know what she's like, lately. It's as though she doesn't want to be a part of this family any more.'

'That's my fault,' Cherry says sadly.

'Only a little bit,' I say. 'I don't suppose you meant to fall for Shay, did you? And he didn't plan to fall for you. Cupid has rotten aim sometimes, that's all. If things had been good between Honey and Shay, there wouldn't have been a problem.'

Cherry shrugs. 'I guess,' she says. 'I can't help thinking about it, though. Back in the summer, when Dad and I first arrived, Honey said something to me about trying to muscle in and take her place. That's not what I was trying to do, not at all, but . . . well, it must look that way to her now.'

I fix the final jam-jar lantern into place. 'Look, Honey's

hacked off about Shay, obviously, but that's just a part of it. She's still struggling to accept Paddy, and she's gutted about Dad moving to Australia . . .'

'We all are,' Coco says. 'Did you know it takes a whole day on a plane just to get there? That sucks!'

'Majorly,' I agree. 'Look on the bright side, though. We'll be able to go out and visit him when we're older. Do a gap year or something.'

'D'you think he'll want us to?' Coco asks.

'Of course!' I say, although I have no idea if that's true.

He's my dad and I love him, but there's no getting round the fact that he is hopeless, and always has been. Even when we were little he was away in London, working, a lot of the time. When he finally moved out, it felt like he had chosen work instead of family, and that hurt.

Only Honey can't seem to admit he's a disaster at being a dad. It seems like she's looking for anyone else to blame but him, and Cherry and Paddy are easy targets.

Just then Summer comes running down the steps towards us, breathless and grinning.

'Guess what?' she says. 'They're going to let me do pointe classes in the New Year! Miss Elise says that I've been doing really well at Intermediate Foundation, and that my feet are strong. She thinks I'm ready. She says I don't have to worry about taking the exam in June because she's going to move me up a class and put me in with the Intermediate lot. She says she has very high hopes of me!'

'That's brilliant, Summer!' I say. 'Wow!'

'Fantastic!' Cherry and Coco chime in.

Dancing on pointe is Summer's dream, and it used to be mine too, before I sussed I had two left feet. Miss Elise, who runs the ballet school in town, may well have 'high hopes' of Summer but she once told me I danced like a fairy elephant. Nice.

'I can get pointe shoes for Christmas,' Summer says, eyes shining. 'Finally!'

'Awesome,' I grin. 'Miss Elise must be really pleased with you to move you up a class too. How cool is that?'

'Pretty cool,' Summer says. 'A bit scary too, though. There's only a handful of girls in the Intermediate class, and all of them are older than me. What if it's too hard?'

'When has anything ballet-related ever been too hard for you?' I tell her. 'My superstar sister!'

*

But later that night as we are getting ready for the party, Summer puts down her hairbrush and sighs.

'Skye . . .?' she starts tentatively. 'Have you ever wanted something so badly you were almost too scared to wish for it?'

I frown. This doesn't sound like my twin.

'Moving up to this class is a lot of pressure,' Summer says. 'It makes me nervous. Everything is going so well, but it just feels so . . . I don't know, fragile. One wrong move and it could all fall to bits.'

I have spent so long admiring Summer's talent for dance – and yes, OK, envying it too – that I've never stopped to imagine how it might feel to be in her shoes.

I don't think her doubts will last more than a moment, though. I know better than anyone how driven my twin can be, how hard she works, how much she loves what she does . . . she'll cope fine.

'Nothing's going to fall to bits,' I tell her. 'Miss Elise wouldn't suggest moving up a class unless she knew you could handle it. You're one of her star pupils, Summer!'

Summer looks unsure, but just as quickly the doubts and shadows vanish. She laughs and pulls the brush through her

❀❀❀❀❀❀❀❀❀❀❀❀❀❀❀❀❀❀❀❀❀❀❀

gleaming hair, confident, determined, in control again.

'I suppose I can't quite believe it,' she tells me. 'All the things I dreamed about, starting to come true!'

'Believe it,' I say, smoothing the skirts of my white cotton petticoats. 'You're going to be a prima ballerina one day, and I will be an archaeologist maybe, or something like that, and we will both be rich and famous!'

'You bet!' Summer laughs.

I slide on an armful of Clara's silver bracelets and lift the emerald-green wool coat out from the old pine trunk, with the faintest waft of marshmallow, quickly gone.

My twin pulls a face. 'You're not wearing that awful coat, are you? Because I can just about see the appeal of the petticoats and the bracelets, but that coat is ancient! And creepy, obviously.'

The closeness I felt for my twin a minute ago dissolves instantly. Sometimes it feels as if I always have to be there for her, yet never the other way round. Can't she try to understand the things that matter to me sometimes too?

'It's vintage,' I say reasonably. 'And warm. And a coat can't be creepy, OK?'

'I don't like it.'

❀❀❀❀❀❀❀❀❀❀❀❀❀❀❀❀❀❀❀❀❀❀

'But I do.' I twirl round so that the heavy fabric spins out around me and a flash of satin lining and cotton lace peeps through.

Clara Travers wore this coat. Did she wear it to walk hand in hand with her fiancé, to go to the theatre, the opera, the ballet? Or did she pull it around her on a cold, dark night to run down to the woods, searching for the flare of golden flames in the darkness, the smell of woodsmoke, the warmth of a boy's hand in hers? For a moment, I'm back in the dream again, in the firelight, watching a boy with blue eyes that take my breath away . . .

I think my imagination is working overtime.

'Please, Skye?' I hear Summer ask, and I snap back to the present. 'I can't explain. I just don't like that coat, OK?'

My twin's face is creased, troubled, and to keep the peace I shrug off the emerald-green coat and hang it on the clothes rail, pulling on a boxy jacket instead.

Summer nods her approval. She takes a fringey blue scarf from her side of the wardrobe and wraps it round my neck, letting the ends trail down behind. 'Perfect,' she says. 'In fact, you can have it. I don't wear it any more.'

59

❀❀❀❀❀❀❀❀❀❀❀❀❀❀❀❀❀❀❀

The scarf's not really my kind of thing, but I thank Summer and tell her I've always liked it. I have – but on her, not me.

Summer rewards me with a smile. But all I can think about is a very different smile, and a boy with wild, dark hair and laughing eyes . . .

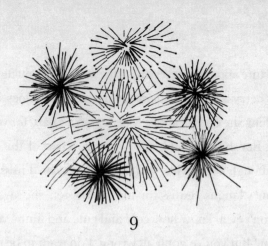

9

Later, I wish I had stuck to my guns and worn the green
coat because it's freezing on the beach. I move closer to the
bonfire, which is roaring, sparks flying out into the velvet-
dark sky.

Paddy sips a bottle of beer and rakes the scarlet embers,
setting foil-wrapped potatoes to bake while Mum ladles
steaming soup into tin mugs. Cherry, Coco and Summer sit
close to the fire, faces bright in the flickering light. Honey
is sitting apart from the rest of us, huddled on the bottom
step of the cliffside path, a sad, shadowy figure in the soft,
pooled light of the lanterns.

I walk across and sink down on to the step beside her.

'I didn't think you'd come,' I say.

'Neither did I,' Honey sighs. 'Mum made such a fuss. This

big lecture about being a part of the family and giving Paddy and Cherry a chance. She really doesn't get it, does she?'

'I think she does,' I shrug. 'She knows it's hard for you. We all do. But she's right, Honey – you are a part of this family, even though you act like you don't want to be. I miss you!'

Honey laughs. 'I miss you too, little sister,' she says. 'I bet you don't even know how cool and cute and funny you are, do you? But you've got it all wrong, I do want to be part of the family . . . I did . . . only Mum and Paddy and Cherry have made that impossible now. They've pushed me out, replaced me. Can't you see that?'

'Nobody could ever replace you,' I say, and it's true – Honey has always been the brightest, boldest, most beautiful sister. She is impulsive, reckless, dramatic, emotional . . . it's what we've always loved about her. But then Dad left, and Paddy and Cherry arrived, and all of the things that once seemed so lovable have begun to turn sour.

'Cherry has,' Honey states coldly. 'She's taken Shay, and she's taken Mum, and she's taken you and Summer and Coco too . . . she has you all fooled, doesn't she? You think she's so sweet –'

'That's not the way it is,' I argue. 'I know she's hurt you,

❀❀❀❀❀❀❀❀❀❀❀❀❀❀❀❀❀❀❀❀

but she didn't plan any of that, and if you actually got to know her –'

'Boy, has she got you suckered,' Honey says. 'Poor little Cherry, with no mum of her own, no sisters, no boyfriend . . . I bet you felt sorry for her, right? Only while you were making her welcome, she moved right in and helped herself to everything she wanted!'

Honey looks across to the bonfire, where Summer, Cherry and Coco are laughing, talking, drinking soup from tin mugs, their faces flickering in the firelight. I see my new stepsister, her confidence growing, starting to feel a part of things; Honey sees a con artist, a liar, a thief.

I don't know if I will ever get her to see things any differently.

Tears brim in Honey's eyes and spill down her cheeks like rain, but when I try to put an arm round her shoulders she shakes me off roughly, jumps to her feet and runs away up the lantern-lit steps towards the house.

Maybe I didn't handle things too well.

Summer appears at my side. 'What did you say to Honey, Skye?' she wants to know. 'She was crying! Why did you have to upset her?'

63

❀❀❀❀❀❀❀❀❀❀❀❀❀❀❀❀❀❀❀❀❀❀

'I didn't . . . I just . . . I was trying to tell her how much we need her, that's all. I said that if she'd just give Cherry a chance . . .'

Summer raises an eyebrow. 'Tactful,' she says. 'The last time Honey gave Cherry a chance, what happened? Cherry stole her boyfriend!'

'It wasn't like that!' I protest.

'Maybe not,' my sister shrugs. 'I bet it looked that way to Honey, though. And you've always made it pretty clear you're on Cherry's side.'

My mouth opens and then closes again, shocked. Summer and I don't argue or wind each other up, not ever. We are always on each other's side, no matter what – or at least we were, until the silly disagreements about Clara's dresses and the emerald-green coat.

'I'm not on anyone's side!' I tell my twin. 'How could I be? Honey is family!'

'I'm guessing she might not feel that way right now,' Summer says.

'Let's not fight,' I say. 'Please, Summer. I just want us all to get along! That's what I was trying to say to Honey.'

My twin sighs. 'Look, Skye,' she says. 'Relax. I wasn't

64

blaming you, just trying to think how Honey might be feeling. Forget I said anything.'

She nudges me, trying to make me smile, but I'm not sure that smiling is an option right now. Nor is forgetting.

'C'mon, Skye, I didn't mean to upset you!'

She hooks an arm round my shoulders and pulls me over to the fire, and my panic begins to fade. Paddy plays the violin, a soft, haunting tune, while Coco, Cherry and I skewer marshmallows on long sharpened sticks and toast them in the bonfire. We eat the marshmallows sticky and smoky and melting hot, a taste like memories.

I gaze into the flames and imagine a boy with a sweet, crooked smile and laughing blue eyes, a boy called Finch. I close my eyes and wish I could conjure up the dream again. It would feel a whole lot less complicated than real life at the moment.

We light sparklers, and Summer winds me up by writing *Alfie* in the air right in front of me, and I use my sparkler to scribble through it before tracing out the name *Finch* when nobody is looking.

Then Paddy lights the fireworks and they begin to rocket skywards, exploding with soft popping sounds, scattering

❀❀❀❀❀❀❀❀❀❀❀❀❀❀❀❀❀❀❀❀❀❀❀

stars across the darkness. As I watch the showering fountains of silver sparks fall back down to earth, I try to shake off the horrible feeling that my family is unravelling. I never fight with anyone, and I've nearly fallen out with my twin . . .

Maybe it's because Summer has had a long day, a tiring day, what with all the changes to her dance schedule. Maybe she's just feeling a little prickly? Millie says that we are full of hormones right now because of growing up, and those hormones can make us moody or sad or tearful for no particular reason.

Whatever just happened between Summer and me, it wasn't anything serious. Was it?

10

Finch is waiting for me beside the gate where the mallow plants arch upwards, waist high, starred with blush-pink flowers with ragged, silken petals. He picks three or four of them, carelessly, and threads them gently into my hair, then takes my hand and leads me down through the woods.

A glimmer of orange flickers through the trees and there's the sound of singing, laughter. I can see the caravans, and there's a flash of swishing skirts, white petticoats, bright stockings, as women dance in the firelight. One man plays a violin, another holds an accordion, squeezing wild, wonderful, wistful sounds from it.

We watch the dancers for a while, stamping our feet and clapping in time to the music, breathing in woodsmoke, watching the sparks fly. When Finch pulls me into the middle of it all, I forget that I don't know the steps, that I don't like dancing. I follow him, knowing I would follow him anywhere, anywhere at all. We laugh and whirl around in the firelight, a girl with flowers in her hair, a boy with laughing eyes, until we are breathless and dizzy, hearts thumping, and not just from the dancing.

I wake in a tangle of duvet, the silver bracelets pressing hard against my cheek. A thin, wintry light trickles through the curtains, and Summer is at the dressing table, plaiting her hair, dressed for ballet practice.

'You missed some great dancing last night,' I say, half asleep still. 'Around the fire.'

'Dancing? What dancing?' my twin asks.

My head struggles to remember. 'Not at the beach bonfire,' I explain. 'Later . . . in the woods. Remember?'

'What are you talking about, Skye?' Summer says. 'We sat by the bonfire for a while after the fireworks, then went to bed . . . there was no dancing.'

I sit up, shivering, put a hand up to my hair where the mallow flowers should be. Nothing. Another dream . . . like the last one, about a boy called Finch, a boy with dark hair and laughing eyes. Gypsy caravans in the woods, music, dancing, and blush-pink mallow flowers even though it is November.

❀❀❀❀❀❀❀❀❀❀❀❀❀❀❀❀❀❀❀❀

It felt so real.

Fear uncurls inside me and my eyes prickle with tears. I fell asleep wearing Clara's bracelets and dreamt myself into her story again . . . at least, that's what it felt like. A gypsy caravan, a boy called Finch, music, dancing, laughter. I love history, but this is a little too close to home. Clara's story has lodged itself inside my head and it's playing tricks with my mind.

'Skye?' Summer says. 'Are you OK?'

I frown. 'Sure . . . I remember now,' I say. 'Must have been a dream . . .'

Summer's eyes widen. 'Skye, you're crying!' She slides an arm round my shoulder and wipes away the tears.

Why am I crying? Because of a girl called Clara Travers, whose love story ended in the cold, wide ocean? Or because of a boy called Finch who makes my heart beat faster, a boy from a whole different century?

It's all too weird.

'Was it a nightmare?' my sister asks.

'No . . . yes . . . I don't know!' I whisper. 'I . . . I think I dreamt about Clara and the gypsies.'

Summer's face is anxious. 'Clara?' she echoes. 'No wonder

69

you're spooked, Skye! You have to let go of it. It's just a stupid old ghost story, right? A load of rubbish.'

'Right,' I say, although I don't believe it. And I am not sure that letting go is an option.

'Now do you see why I think you should ditch the old clothes?' Summer asks. 'It's just creepy, the way you're always wearing her stuff! It's not worth it if it gives you nightmares!'

She slides the silver bracelets from my wrist and dumps them into the trunk, shutting the lid firmly. 'OK?' she says. 'Ditch the clothes. Promise? No more nightmares!'

'I guess . . .' I say. 'I promise . . .'

'Summer!' Mum calls up the stairs. 'Are you ready? We're going to be late!'

Summer grabs her dance kit.

'Sorry, Skye. I have to go. It's the auditions for the Christmas show today.'

'Right,' I say. 'Good luck then.'

She flashes me a smile and is gone.

I rake a hand through my hair. It's almost eleven, too late to help with the guest breakfasts, but in a little while, when Mum gets back, I'll help her with the room changes. Right now, my mind is reeling.

70

I've promised Summer, but already I know it's a promise I can't keep.

I don't *want* to let go of Clara's story. It scares me, but more than that, it fascinates me too. I just wish I knew what it all meant. It's as though the dreams are pulling me back to the 1920s, to a time when gypsy travellers camped out in the woods, to another world – yet it feels so real, so right. It feels like my world.

I look out of the window, my eyes following the stone wall that separates our garden from the woods. I can just make out the little gate from my dream, but the paint is peeling with age and the mallow plants are dying back now in the first autumn frosts. There are no flowers left, but I know the name of the plant because Mum picks the soft pink flowers in late summer to sprinkle over salads.

'Marshmallow used to be a medicinal herb,' she told me once. 'It's what the sweets used to be made from, once upon a time. The flowers are edible – not all flowers are, but these are so pretty in a salad or on top of a cupcake . . .'

I liked the idea that my favourite sweet came originally from a pretty garden herb, even then.

71

❀❀❀❀❀❀❀❀❀❀❀❀❀❀❀❀❀❀

In the dream, Finch put mallow flowers in my hair . . . does that mean that Clara liked them too?

I don't believe in ghosts, I really don't, but what if it's not about clanking chains and unearthly howls and white-faced spectres that glide through walls? What if a haunting can be gentler, less scary?

I run my fingers over the white cotton lace of Clara's petticoat. For almost a hundred years it lay folded, forgotten, in a wooden trunk in the corner of the attic, until Paddy found it. Was it coincidence? Was it just luck the trunk found its way to me, a girl hooked on vintage clothes and stories of the past?

It has to be, I know, but the dreams make me wonder.

I open up the wooden trunk, push aside velvet dresses, cloche hats, a beaded clutch bag, looking for clues. There is nothing ghostly or sinister, nothing to suggest that the trunk holds secrets or mysteries. There is no dark force pulling me back towards the past, no blast of icy air, nothing but a collection of old dresses and petticoats, the clutch bag with its intricate beadwork, as perfect as if it was made last week and not last century.

I glimpse the bundle of letters tied with ribbon. Why didn't I think of these before? There might be clues in them.

I set them down on my desk among the clutter of school-books and magazines and pens and paintboxes, to read later.

Then I go back to the trunk and take out the clutch bag, snapping open the clasp. I catch my breath. Inside is a scarlet lipstick, a silver powder compact with butterflies on the lid, and a tiny bottle of square-cut glass holding just a trickle of perfume. I unscrew the lid and breathe in the fragrance, marshmallow sweet and yet cleaner, lighter, fresher than my favourite treat. Marshmallow. Was it Clara's favourite too? And then the smell is gone, replaced by something heavy, cloying, stale.

I guess perfume doesn't last across the decades after all. I prise open the compact. The mirror inside is clouded with age, but inside the lid is a message, engraved for all to see.

For Clara, my beautiful girl, your loving Harry.

Harry. The name of Clara's fiancé.

How many times did Clara hold this powder compact in her hands, gaze into its mirror to dust her face pale or colour her lips red? Every single time, she would have seen that message. Did it make her heart leap, to begin with? Or did she feel heavy with the secret knowledge that she didn't love him back?

❀❀❀❀❀❀❀❀❀❀❀❀❀❀❀❀❀❀❀❀❀❀❀

I click the compact shut.

There is one more thing inside the clutch bag, half hidden in a fold of satin lining. It slides into my palm like a talisman: a small silver locket shaped like a heart, tarnished grey with age but still beautiful with its intricate tracery of pattern curling and curving beneath my touch.

The catch springs open at the first attempt, and I bite my lip. Inside the locket is a photograph, a small sepia picture of a man in old-fashioned evening dress, with serious eyes and a neat moustache.

Harry looks like someone's stern uncle, not the boyfriend of a seventeen-year-old girl. And not one single bit like the dark-haired gypsy boy from my dream.

11

Summer comes home full of smiles because not only has she has been given a good role in the dance school's Christmas production but also a job as student helper to one of the younger classes.

'It's usually the older girls who get to do that,' she says, eyes shining. 'It's quite a big thing to be asked, and of course, it means extra dances and routines to learn. It's only six weeks until the show. Hardly any time at all!'

'What did I say?' I grin. 'My sister, the superstar!'

'Hardly,' she says. 'Not yet, anyhow!'

Summer doesn't mention Clara again and I don't remind her, and that is a very good thing because my twin can still see right into my heart, my soul, if she really wants to. She would definitely suss out a promise just waiting to be broken.

❀❀❀❀❀❀❀❀❀❀❀❀❀❀❀❀❀❀❀❀❀❀❀

Right now, I'd rather she didn't.

The dreams wrap themselves around my heart, my mind, a secret I'm not willing to let go of.

Lately, school has become a game of hide-and-seek with me hiding and Alfie seeking. Even though I know he has the hots for some mystery girl, everyone else seems to think he is crushing on me. I am teased endlessly, which is no fun at all.

'He likes you,' Millie sighs. 'Definitely. You could go out with him, Skye, because he is not actually ugly or anything, and you might not have a better offer for ages . . .'

When your best friend says something like that, you know you are in trouble.

We are in the school canteen. Alfie is at a nearby table, juggling satsumas and flicking chips at his mates, and we are sitting in a corner, half hidden behind a pillar and hoping he won't spot us. I'm hoping, anyhow.

'I just don't fancy him, Millie,' I say patiently.

'It doesn't have to be true love,' she shrugs. 'But you will be thirteen in February, and face it, you have never had a boyfriend –'

'Neither have you!' I protest.

❀❀❀❀❀❀❀❀❀❀❀❀❀❀❀❀❀❀❀❀❀

'I know,' Millie says. 'It's depressing. I would go out with Alfie Anderson in a heartbeat, if he asked me.'

'You would?' I ask, incredulous. 'Last week on the bus you were making pukey faces behind his back!'

Millie shrugs. 'Things change. We have to be realistic. I've been thinking about it, and I've decided he would make a very good starter boyfriend.'

'Starter boyfriend?' I echo. 'You're kidding me, right? Alfie Anderson has the haircut of a deranged lunatic and the personality of an over-excited puppy. He means well, but he's not house-trained, and that's kind of exhausting.'

Millie frowns. 'You don't get this, do you?' she says. 'I don't fancy him either. That's not the point. I'm just saying, he is a boy, and not totally disgusting, and we need to think about boyfriends soon, Skye, or we will be left on the shelf. Old and shrivelled and past our sell-by date.'

'You make us sound like a couple of mouldy old prunes,' I say.

'That's what we'll be, if we don't do something,' Millie insists. 'We need to get out there, get dating. Otherwise, how will we know what to do when the boy of our dreams comes along?'

❀❀❀❀❀❀❀❀❀❀❀❀❀❀❀❀❀❀❀❀❀❀❀❀

I bite my lip. The boy of my dreams is taking up a little too much of my thoughts lately, but the chances of me bumping into Finch on Kitnor High Street are pretty slim. The only explanation I have for him so far is that he's a kind of dream version of the gyspy boy Clara Travers fell for, which means the chances of me bumping into him anywhere are slim, unless we are talking séances and time travel. Somehow, freakily, I seem to be dreaming Clara's memories, her story. I meant to start reading through Clara's letters to try to work it out, but I got distracted the other day and when I looked for them again they weren't where I'd left them.

I remind myself to look for them properly; I have to unravel the mystery.

'I don't want a boyfriend,' I say firmly now. 'And especially not Alfie Anderson.'

'You love him really,' Summer says, gliding up behind me and swiping the grapes from my fruit salad. 'Don't try to fight it.'

Tia flops down into a seat beside Millie, winks at me and blows a kiss at Alfie. Luckily, he is too busy clowning around to notice.

'You're not funny,' I say.

'You are,' Summer grins. 'You're just so easy to wind up! Relax, we know you're not interested in Alfie. Who would be?'

'I think he's got potential,' Millie says thoughtfully.

'I think he's got jam all over his face,' Tia adds.

I glance across at Alfie, who is trying to stuff an entire sponge pudding into his mouth at once, and sigh. If there is potential there, I can't quite see it.

Alfie spots us watching him and turns a dark shade of red before wiping his face, gulping down the sponge pudding and sitting down quietly. I know he doesn't fancy me, but it's just possible that Tia or Millie might be his secret crush girl. Well, maybe not Millie, because Alfie wasn't exactly friendly to her on the school bus the other day, but that could have been an attempt to hide his true feelings, couldn't it?

I think he probably does need some advice. On using less hair gel and less Lynx bodyspray and not stuffing so much cake into his mouth that he looks like a demented hamster streaked with strawberry jam. I could help him.

It would be a kind thing to do, like picking up litter from the side of the road, or knitting blankets for earthquake

❁❁❁❁❁❁❁❁❁❁❁❁❁❁❁❁❁❁❁❁❁❁

victims, or having a cake sale to raise money for endangered species.

'He *definitely* likes you,' Summer whispers.

Spots of pink flare in my cheeks, but I pretend not to care. 'Trust me, he doesn't,' I say firmly. 'Maybe it's one of you lot?'

'Oh!' Millie gasps. 'Do you think so?'

'Ugh,' Tia huffs.

'As long as it's not me,' Summer says. 'I just don't see what all the fuss is about boys. I mean, there might be one or two reasonable boys in our year, but Alfie is not one of them. Romance is over-rated. I am going to focus on my dance career, unless I happen to meet Rudolf Nureyev, of course . . .'

'Not sure that's going to happen,' Millie says. 'Rudolf Nureyev is dead. And gay. And frankly, men in tights are a definite turn-off.'

'You'd be surprised,' my twin says darkly, and flounces off to the salad bar.

'I thought you were the history nut, not Summer?' Tia says. 'Falling for a guy who's been dead for decades sounds more like your kind of trick!'

❀❀❀❀❀❀❀❀❀❀❀❀❀❀❀❀❀❀❀❀❀❀

I can't help smiling because Tia has a point. After all, I feel like I am falling for someone who could've been dead for decades too . . . or someone who doesn't exist at all, and whichever way you look at it, that's pretty weird.

I don't care, though. Finch may not be real, but he is whole lot cooler than the boys at Exmoor Park Middle School, and way better-looking too.

When Alfie finally corners me after history, I have no energy left to argue. I think of him with jam on his face, his tie askew, and find myself agreeing to meet him at the weekend so that we can talk 'in private'.

'I'll buy the milkshakes,' he says brightly.

'Make it hot chocolate with marshmallows and you might have a deal,' I sigh.

'Done,' Alfie grins.

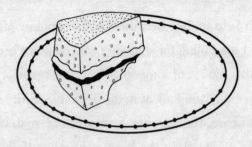

12

So that's how I end up in the Mad Hatter on Saturday, sitting opposite Alfie Anderson, spooning up hot chocolate and soft, chewy marshmallows topped with cream. He has chosen the window seat, which feels a bit public really, but I pull my cloche hat a little lower and try not to mind.

'OK, Skye, I need your help,' he says. 'You are a girl, so you might be able to tell me where I've been going wrong. I have a plan, and you can help me make it happen. The thing is . . . I want to be irresistible to women.'

I choke on my hot chocolate, snorting in a very unlady-like way.

Alfie's cheeks glow pink. 'What?' he asks, sounding a little hurt. 'Is that funny or something?'

'No, no,' I assure him. 'I wasn't laughing. It's just that

some of my hot chocolate went down the wrong way . . .'

'Yeah, right,' Alfie sulks. 'That is exactly the problem. I am crushing on a girl who thinks I am a complete idiot, and it hurts, so I figured I should do some homework on what girls are actually looking for in a boy. I don't actually spend much time with girls, apart from my little sisters. They are a bit of a mystery to me. And obviously, we have been friends forever, so who better to ask than you?'

Friends forever? I'm not sure that's how I'd describe it . . . although I vaguely recall he was at the last big birthday party Summer and I had, when we were nine, the year Dad left. He ate all the sausage rolls, most of the trifle, and at least half a dozen chocolate cupcakes, and ended up being sick in the bathroom. He did give us a packet of Rolos each as presents, but he must have got hungry on the way because half of mine were missing.

Alfie takes out a notepad and pen and looks at me expectantly.

'You're taking notes?' I ask. 'Seriously?'

'It's a very serious problem,' he says. 'Like I said, there is this girl I like. I have liked her for quite a while, but she thinks I am an idiot.'

❀❀❀❀❀❀❀❀❀❀❀❀❀❀❀❀❀❀❀❀❀❀

Got to be Tia, I think. I am not sure there is any hope for Alfie's crush.

'Is there anywhere you can see where I might be going wrong?' he asks. 'Any tips?'

I sigh. 'OK then – hair,' I begin. 'Ditch the straighteners and the gel. You look like a maniac.'

'But . . . I got this look out of a fashion mag!' he protests. 'It takes me half an hour every morning to get right!'

'That's just it – I'm not sure you *are* getting it right,' I say patiently. 'You look like you've ironed your fringe in about seven different directions, then had a fight with a tub of gel and a can of hairspray. Trust me, it's not a good look. Ditch it – stay in bed for an extra half-hour. Go for the natural look.'

'OK,' he says, scribbling in the notebook. 'Anything else?'

'You need to dredge up a few manners. Like this week, with the sponge pudding at school . . . that was kind of distressing. Slow down a little. Eat your food, don't wear it!'

Alfie grins. 'I can do that,' he says. 'Definitely.'

'And no more clowning around in class,' I add. 'That's important. It's . . . well, kind of childish. You are thirteen now, right? Practical jokes just aren't that funny any more.'

Alfie's eyes widen. 'But . . . everyone laughs!' he argues. 'They expect it of me! I am the class joker!'

'I thought you wanted to be the class Romeo?'

He frowns.

'What would happen if you stopped the messing about?' I ask. 'You would have less detentions, get more work done, spend less time sitting outside Mr King's office writing lines. Teachers would like you. People would take you more seriously. And that is exactly what they're not doing at the moment, right?'

'Girls?' Alfie checks.

'Well . . . maybe,' I shrug.

'But I thought girls liked funny boys?' he questions. 'Making someone laugh is supposed to be a good thing, isn't it? Besides, I am going to be a stand-up comedian one day. It's probably my only talent!'

'You have lots of talents!' I say kindly. 'Probably. Just . . . maybe not comedy. You need people to laugh *with* you, not at you. I think there's more to you than class clown.'

Alfie stares gloomily down at the remnants of the cake he has just demolished. 'Maybe I could be a chef?'

'Maybe,' I agree. 'Whatever you decide to do – you are

❀❀❀❀❀❀❀❀❀❀❀❀❀❀❀❀❀❀❀❀❀❀❀

an OK person, Alfie Anderson, underneath all the jokes and the messing about.'

It's true . . . there is a kind, caring side to Alfie if you take the time to look for it. I think that Millie is right, that he has potential, and that one day, not too far from now, he might make someone a pretty neat boyfriend. As long as it's not me, of course.

Someone raps on the window and I just about jump out of my skin – it's Coco and a bunch of her friends, pulling silly faces and laughing themselves stupid.

'Get lost!' I yell, trying to hide behind the menu, and eventually she gets fed up and drifts away.

'Have your sisters been giving you a hard time?' Alfie grins. 'Summer too?'

'She's the worst,' I admit. 'She thinks it's hugely funny, you hanging around me and talking to me on the bus. And you have to admit, to outsiders, this could look a little bit like a date. You haven't actually done anything to make it clear to people that it's not. It's like you *want* them to think there's something going on!'

Alfie grins. 'Well, it won't do my reputation any harm to be seen out with you, will it?'

'Alfie! I do not want to be part of your "irresistible to women" project. OK?'

'OK,' he laughs. 'So. About Summer . . . you were saying . . . maybe she's just a bit jealous?'

'Er . . . no, I don't think so!' I say.

His face falls, and that's when the penny drops.

He is not crushing on Tia at all.

I understand now why Alfie tagged along with us on Halloween, why he cut the clowning so fast, the day of Mr Wolfe and the broken window. This is why he went pink in the school canteen, embarrassed to be caught with jam on his face. And this is why I am the perfect person to ask for advice, because of course, I know my twin sister better than anyone else alive.

Alfie's mystery girl is Summer.

I just can't work out why that seems to hurt so much.

13

I'm sitting on the caravan steps in the sunshine, beside a boy with sun-brown skin and laughing eyes and a red neckerchief. Dark wavy hair falls across his cheek in unruly waves, and I want to reach out and touch it, but I don't, of course. Finch takes my hand and the silver bracelets jangle, and he leans close, so close that I can smell woodsmoke on his hair . . .

I'm woken up by a huge bang from downstairs, and the dream crashes abruptly. It's Sunday morning, I remember – but normally it's not this . . . loud.

'Something's going on,' Summer says from the doorway. 'Quick!'

When I get down to the kitchen, Paddy is picking up pieces of broken plate and Fred the dog is hoovering up bacon and everyone else is gathered round the table, looking at a glossy magazine.

'Look!' Summer yelps. 'Look at this! You won't believe it!'

'It's us!' Coco cuts in. 'We're famous!'

I lean in to look, and there on the pages of the Sunday paper's magazine are pictures of us, taken in the summer at the Chocolate Festival we staged to launch the Chocolate Box business. The feature is titled *The Chocolate Box*, and there are four bright pages of festival photos along with the feature. There are the chocolates, piled up in little pyramids beside the handpainted boxes that give the business its name. There is the bunting hanging from the treetops, the stalls, the chocolate cafe, the gypsy caravan, the crowds of people. There are Mum and Paddy, smiling into the camera, holding boxes of truffles.

And there we are, Honey, Coco, Cherry, Summer and me, dressed in our cute little chocolate fairy costumes, all brown velvet and golden-brown tutu skirts and little wings, standing together in the dappled sunlight. The tagline on the photo reads *The Chocolate Box Girls*.

'Wow!' I breathe. 'It's the national paper – not just the *Gazette*!'

89

'We look great!' Cherry says. 'Like proper sisters!'

'We are proper sisters,' I tell her. 'Definitely.'

It was only a few months ago, but in that picture we look happy, hopeful and together, in a way we really haven't been since. Honey's wavy golden hair is still waist-length, glinting in the light. Back then she still had Shay, of course – or thought she did. And Dad wasn't living on the other side of the planet. It's not just Honey either – Summer and I are grinning, leaning against each other. There were no fallouts, no secrets, and no broken promises between us back then.

'It's great publicity,' Mum is saying. 'And the write-up is just as good as the photos . . . it talks about the truffles being handmade, and the boxes handpainted. Best of all, it says they taste amazing!'

'Well, they do!' I shrug. 'They're awesome!'

Paddy finishes clearing up the broken plates and comes over to join us, his smile a mile wide.

'Pure brilliant,' he says in his soft Glaswegian accent. 'The feature mentions it all – the B&B, the chocolate business – and lists all the websites too! The Chocolate Festival got the business off to a good start, but things have been

❀❀❀❀❀❀❀❀❀❀❀❀❀❀❀❀❀❀❀❀❀❀

pretty quiet since then. This should give us the boost we really need.'

'I hope so,' Mum says, grinning. 'The timing is perfect. This could make our Christmas!'

I'm relieved – I know that Mum and Paddy have been struggling with money. This could really help.

'I thought those pictures were for the local newspaper, though,' Cherry says, baffled. 'The *Gazette* did a feature ages ago, didn't they?'

'The reporter mentioned that she'd like to pitch it to one of the Sunday papers,' Mum recalls. 'I didn't expect anything would actually come of it, though! Can we cope, if we do have lots of orders?'

'No worries,' Paddy says. 'We'll do it.'

There's a timid knock, and one of the B&B guests puts his head round the kitchen door.

'Sorry to interrupt,' he says. 'It's just that we're still waiting for our bacon and eggs!'

Mum's hands fly up to her face. 'I dropped it!' she admits. 'It was the shock! I'm so sorry . . . I'll be right with you.'

She runs over to the fridge and pulls out fresh supplies,

91

while Paddy shows the bemused guest the Sunday supplement magazine and sends him back into the guest breakfast room clutching it. By the time Mum has produced two more cooked breakfasts and a round of toast, Paddy has headed off to the village to buy more copies of the newspaper.

I take the guest breakfasts through – better late than never.

After that, business really does start to pick up. Orders flood in, by mail, by phone, by email. People stop us in the street and ask if we can do them a special box of truffles for a birthday or anniversary, and Paddy is spending long hours in the workshop making sure the orders are filled and ready to send out. We still have some handpainted boxes left over from the Chocolate Festival, but Mum is working on a new range for the Christmas orders.

Cherry and Honey get lots of comments at the high school, and people keep telling Honey she should be a model. She dumps Alex, the motorbike boy, for an arty Year Twelve lad who wants to photograph her for his portfolio. She has such a hectic social life that it's starting to feel like she is one of the B&B guests, only not quite as friendly and much less likely to appear for breakfast. We hardly ever see her.

Even at Exmoor Park Middle School, Summer, Coco and I are minor celebrities, for a few days at least. We are not the Tanberry sisters any more – we are the Chocolate Box Girls, and there are lots of jokes about tutus and fairy wings.

The teachers get in on the act too, and Paddy sends in a big box of sample chocolates for the staffroom. By the end of the day we have taken seven new orders. Mr Wolfe orders a box for his girlfriend, which makes us giggle.

'Even Mr Wolfe has a girlfriend,' Millie says, shaking her head. 'Unreal. Don't you ever feel like life is passing you by?'

'Er . . . no,' I reply.

'We should go to town on Saturday,' Millie ploughs on. 'All of us. You and me and Summer and Tia. It'd be cool. We could try on clothes and check out the make-up testers in Boots and hang out in the new cafe on the Esplanade. Loads of kids go in there, it's supposed to be really cool. And you and Summer are kind of famous now, so I bet people would recognize you. Boys might come over and chat us up! Older boys, from the high school!'

One of the things I have always liked about Millie is her enthusiasm – whatever she's into, she really goes for it, whether it's ballet, or Barbie dolls, or ponies, or vampire books. This whole boys thing is the same – but it's starting to get a bit full-on.

'I doubt it,' I say to her. 'I can't, anyway, not this Saturday. I promised Paddy I'd help him with the chocolate orders. You can come over and help too, if you want. Besides, I am not interested in boys, you know that!'

'Skye, you are no fun any more!' Millie huffs. 'I bet Summer and Tia would go!'

'Summer's got a ballet class,' I shrug.

'Bor-ing,' Millie grumbles, but she drops the subject. I'm starting to think my best friend is morphing into someone I don't actually know any more. Not so long ago she'd have jumped at the chance to help with the chocolate making, but these days she is obsessed with boys and make-up and whether she will ever be kissed.

And, even though there's one special boy I think about a lot myself, I think Millie's obsession is kind of boring, actually.

14

A boy with dark, wavy hair and a red neckerchief is sitting in the dappled sunlight beneath the hazel trees, when out of nowhere a bird swoops down, a quick flash of brown and red. It lands on the ground in front of him, head to one side, chirping softly. The boy stretches out his hand slowly and the bird hops on, and I hold my breath, enchanted.

Then the bird is gone. Finch looks up at me, grinning, and my heart is racing . . .

I learn to keep the dreams to myself, but some days it is a struggle to come back to the real world. I never used to sleep in, but lately even the radio alarm doesn't always wake me and Summer has to shake me and pull the duvet back so that the cold air rushes in and brings me back to reality.

The truth is, reality is losing its appeal.

Every day I choose something from Clara's trunk to wear, one of the cotton petticoats or the bracelets or the little cloche hat. I am getting hooked on 1920s style, hooked on Clara's clothes, and when I wear them I feel close to her, and more importantly, close to the dream – to Finch.

'You're not still having those spooky dreams, are you?' Summer asks on Saturday morning. She has just woken me up (again), before she dashes off to her ballet class. 'About Clara? Only you're miles away, these days. Distracted.'

My twin's face is anxious, disapproving, and my reaction is instant – protect, conceal, deny.

'Dreams?' I echo. 'What dreams?'

It's not exactly a lie.

Sometimes I look in the mirror, my face shadowed beneath the cloche hat, and think I catch a glimpse of some-one else, a girl from long ago. Sometimes, I even think the girl is trying to tell me something. I remember Clara's letters – weirdly, I never found them. I decide to look for them again – at the moment they're my only hope of finding some clues to what the dreams mean.

Part of me doesn't want to question it all too closely, in case the dreams evaporate, but another part of me needs to know whether it's Clara who's trying to tell me something . . . or just my own imagination, conjuring up a boy who's too good to be true.

I look again all morning until I have to help Mum with the B&B cleaning, but the letters are nowhere to be found. At lunchtime we are sitting round the kitchen table eating tomato soup and freshly baked bread rolls, when Summer gets back from ballet. I know she won't like me asking, but I have to know.

'Summer, you know those old letters from the trunk?' I ask. 'Have you seen them at all? I left them on the desk a week or so ago and they seem to have vanished into thin air . . .'

'What letters?' Summer says blankly.

'You know . . . the bundle of letters addressed to Clara Travers. I thought you might have moved them or something.'

Summer frowns. 'I don't know . . . I might have put them back in the trunk . . .'

'They're not there, though,' I sigh. 'I've looked. Could you have put them somewhere else?'

97

Summer looks annoyed. 'Look, I can't remember – I probably didn't move them at all, Skye. Why would I touch her spooky old letters?'

'I don't know,' I shrug. 'I'm not blaming you, Summer, it's just that I've lost them and it's bugging me, that's all. Mum . . . have you seen the letters from the trunk? Tidied them up or something?'

'I don't know, love,' she says. 'Sorry. I don't think so – but to be honest we're so manic with the chocolate orders it's all I can do to keep on top of the B&B stuff lately. I haven't tidied your rooms in a while. We're busier with guests as well as the Chocolate Box, thanks to that article.'

'If things stay this way after Christmas, we might have to look into employing an assistant,' Paddy comments.

'Wow,' Coco grins. 'That's a good sign, isn't it?'

'Brilliant,' Mum agrees. 'Right now, though, we're run off our feet. I don't know what we'd do without your help, girls!'

We've got into a routine of helping out in the workshop after school, assembling boxes and selecting chocolates and tying up the ribbon bows. Then we slide them into jiffy bags and Paddy takes everything down to the post office in time

❀❀❀❀❀❀❀❀❀❀❀❀❀❀❀❀❀❀❀❀❀❀❀❀

to catch the last pickup, and we get to eat any leftover truffles. Obviously, that is the best bit.

Honey, who has made a rare lunchtime appearance, rolls her eyes. 'It's child labour,' she says scathingly. 'We do enough already, helping Mum with the guest rooms and breakfasts. What are we, slaves?'

'You haven't helped with the B&B stuff for ages,' I say. 'So *you* are definitely not a slave, anyway. The rest of us don't mind. It's fun!'

'You think?' Summer asks. I know she is only sticking up for Honey, but it's not like my twin actually helps out as much as the rest of us anyhow. She always has ballet practice or dance-show rehearsal or something. Cherry, Coco and I do most of the work, and we are not complaining.

'A few more chocolate orders won't help us much anyhow.' Honey shrugs. 'How many thousands do you owe the bank again, Paddy?'

'Actually . . .' Paddy begins, but my big sister ignores him.

'When the business falls flat on its face, how are you going to pay the debt?' she demands. 'Maybe you won't. Maybe you'll leave Mum to sort that out –'

'Honey!' Mum snaps. 'That's enough!'

99

Paddy sighs. 'She's only trying to watch out for you,' he says patiently. 'You can't really blame her for that.'

'If it makes her rude, I can,' Mum sighs. 'I wish I could believe that Honey was just watching out for me, but sometimes I think she just likes to stir up trouble –'

'Er, hello?' Honey cuts in. 'Who's being rude now? You're talking about me as if I'm not even here.'

'You hardly ever are,' I say, and Summer shoots me an angry look. She is fiercely loyal to Honey – but surely even she can see now that our big sister is out to make trouble?

'Enough,' Mum says. 'If business stays brisk we'll look into employing an assistant in the spring, but right now your help is much appreciated, all of you. That's what families do – help each other. It won't be for long, but we're up to our eyes at the moment, what with trying to get your new sister's bedroom finished off as well –'

Mum's comment is like a red rag to a bull. I see Honey's eyes flash with anger.

'Cherry will never be my sister . . . wedding or no wedding,' she bites out. 'And right now, my money's on no wedding.'

'Honey, don't be so mean!' I argue. It's not like me to get

❀❀❀❀❀❀❀❀❀❀❀❀❀❀❀❀❀❀❀❀❀❀❀

in the middle of a family drama, but I feel so sorry for Mum, and for Cherry, I have to say something. 'Don't you want Mum to be happy again, after everything Dad put her through? Don't you want to be a part of this family?'

Honey glares at me, her blue eyes icy cold.

'My family fell apart,' she bites out. 'A while ago now. I thought we could put it back together, but I was wrong, because you all had other ideas. Now I'm stuck with a whole different set-up, and no, I don't want to be a part of it, Skye, now that you ask.'

I feel like I've been slapped.

An awkward silence settles around us. Paddy's bright smile slips and Cherry looks down at her soup bowl as if she would like to be anywhere at all but here. The rest of us struggle for a way out of the embarrassment, a way to put it all right, but there isn't one.

It strikes me suddenly that I do not like my big sister very much at all. I'm sick of creeping around her, trying to coax a smile or a friendly word. I'm sick of trying to be the peacemaker because if she saw a white flag she'd most likely tear it in two. Honey is pulling my family to pieces.

'You never used to be like this,' I say quietly. 'I used to

look up to you, Honey, you know? I thought you were the coolest big sister in the world, but I was wrong. You're not cool at all . . . you're shallow and spiteful and cruel!'

'Skye, hush!' Mum says, but it's too late – Honey is on her feet, her lips trembling, eyes misted with tears. She slams out of the kitchen and runs up the stairs to her room.

15

I stood up to my sister and told her the things that have been whirling around in my head, but instead of feeling better I feel as if I am the one in the wrong. Sadness settles inside my chest like a stone.

Summer digs me in the ribs. 'What did you have to go and say that for?' she whispers. 'She'll be even worse now!'

I bite my lip. 'I just . . . I couldn't believe she'd say that stuff . . . oh, I don't know. I'm sorry!'

Mum sighs. 'Maybe you actually got through to her? I'm not getting things right with Honey at the moment, I know that. Perhaps we need to take a harder line . . . for her own sake.'

'Worth a try,' Paddy nods. 'And, Skye, I think it's good

you challenged her. Maybe it'll be the wake-up call she needs?'

'Maybe,' I say, but I don't believe it, not really. I don't think Honey wants a wake-up call. And what if Summer is right, and my words push her still further away?

My twin shoots me a cold look and heads off to the village to meet Tia for a trip into town. I head out to help in the workshop with Cherry, Coco and Paddy, but I can't focus and end up getting the orders wrong. I keep thinking of Honey's eyes, misted with tears, of Summer's accusing glare. I feel like the worst sister in the world.

When Paddy suggests I take some packages down to the post office and then call in at the bakery to buy cream cakes for tea, I jump at the chance.

I am in the post office handing over a whole heap of parcels when Mrs Lee, the post office lady, stops what she is doing and stares at me, hard. Mrs Lee is pretty eccentric, and styles herself as some kind of gypsy fortune-teller. She has been telling me that I'm a little bit psychic ever since I was six years old, which used to make me feel very important and special because she never said anything like that to Summer.

❀❀❀❀❀❀❀❀❀❀❀❀❀❀❀❀❀❀❀❀

She's always coming out with some crazy prediction, which can be very unsettling when you've only gone in to buy a second-class stamp or a roll of Sellotape.

'Skye, I'm sensing a sadness about you today . . . am I right?' Mrs Lee says.

'I'm not in a great mood, if that's what you mean,' I sigh.

'It's more than that, though, isn't it, pet? There's something on your mind. You look . . . haunted.'

'What d'you mean?' I squeak. I'm used to Mrs Lee, but that's a bit close to home. 'There's no such thing as ghosts!' I say shakily.

'Who knows?' she says. 'There are a lot of things out there we don't fully understand . . . shadows from the past . . . echoes of unhappiness and sorrow from long ago. Those things are real enough, Skye, and tragedies can leave their mark on the present day. I've seen it again and again. For sensitive people, those with a sixth sense, an empathy with the past – like you and me, Skye – well, maybe ghosts aren't as far-fetched as the scientists make out!'

My mind floods with possibilities. I'd almost forgotten about Clara and the letters what with all the drama at home, but Mrs Lee has brought it all back. Could I be tuning in to some kind of sadness from the past, something that surfaces in my dreams? Are sorrow and unhappiness folded around the velvet dresses and cotton petticoats just like the lingering marshmallow fragrance?

But I don't think it can be that. The dreams don't feel sad or scary, just the opposite. It's tearing myself away from that world that is the challenge. Perhaps the clothes a girl once wore can hold on to some of her energy, some of her memories, even years and years later . . . but if the clothes were heavy with sadness and pain, wouldn't I be able to feel that too, if I really am as sensitive as Mrs Lee says?

I blink, and Mrs Lee laughs. 'That's not actually what I meant, though, pet . . . I was just saying, you look upset. Haunted, you know. It was just an expression!'

Colour floods my cheeks. 'Of course,' I mumble. 'Obviously. I had a fallout with my sister . . .'

Two of my sisters, actually.

'Ah,' Mrs Lee says, weighing and stamping the packages. 'Families . . . they're complicated things, Skye. People say and do things they regret.'

I push a couple of notes across the counter to pay, but Mrs Lee ignores the cash and picks up my hand, turning it

❀❀❀❀❀❀❀❀❀❀❀❀❀❀❀❀❀❀❀❀

over to study the palm. I am very glad there is nobody else in the post office.

'Goodness,' she says. 'You're growing up so fast, Skye. I see romance!'

I laugh. 'I don't think so . . .'

Mrs Lee purses her lips. 'I'm never wrong,' she says huffily. 'I have the gift, you know. I learnt how to read palms from my mum. She was half Romany gypsy!'

'OK,' I grin. 'I'm sorry! Only I am not all that interested in boys, really.'

Unless they are boys like Finch, of course, but they don't exist outside my dreams, I am pretty sure of that.

'Perhaps you haven't met him yet,' Mrs Lee concedes, frowning. 'But he's here, all right . . . clear as day. I'm seeing something else too . . .' She peers more closely at my palm. 'A small bird? A finch, maybe?'

I pull my hand away as if I've been burnt.

Finch. A dream boy, a boy who must have lived almost a hundred years ago . . . if he existed at all.

This is way too weird, too freaky.

If Mrs Lee is right – how can a boy who belongs to the past be a part of my future?

❀❀❀❀❀❀❀❀❀❀❀❀❀❀❀❀❀❀❀❀❀

Mrs Lee counts out my change and I take my receipt and run all the way to the bakery, where I try to pull myself together. I pick out cream cakes for everyone, including Honey's favourite – a chocolate eclair – and I'm just on my way out, balancing the two boxes carefully, when I am ambushed by Alfie Anderson. Possibly the last person on earth I want to see right now.

'Skye,' he says cheerfully. 'How's it going? I'd buy you a milkshake, only I've got no money . . .'

'I'd buy you a Porsche, only I don't have any money either,' I sigh, and Alfie laughs and falls into step beside me.

'Playpark?' he suggests. 'We can scare the little kids away and hang upside down from the top of the swings and run up the shiny bit of the slide instead of sliding down it . . .'

'Alfie, it's cold,' I point out. 'And it'll be getting dark soon.'

And I do not especially want to be seen in public with a dodgy boy who is in love with my perfect twin. I want to be alone, to pick over the weird stuff Mrs Lee was saying, to work out how come a ghost boy is written in my palm, and how I'm going to patch things up with Honey and Summer.

'Please?' he persists.

'Alfie, seriously, there is no way . . .'

❀❀❀❀❀❀❀❀❀❀❀❀❀❀❀❀❀❀❀❀❀❀❀

I may as well save my breath. Five minutes later we are sitting on the roundabout in the playpark, which just goes to show that some days are doomed.

I huddle on the roundabout trying to keep warm and guarding my boxes of cream cakes while Alfie spins it faster and faster. Just when we get to the point where I think my head might explode he stops and flops down beside me.

'So,' he says as the world spins by around us. 'What do you want for Christmas then?'

I roll my eyes. 'Christmas is ages away!'

'Actually, it's four weeks and two days away,' he corrects me. 'Not long at all. We're getting our Christmas tree next weekend!'

'I think we are too,' I say. 'We've had a fake one for the last few years, but Paddy says he's going to find us the biggest tree in Somerset.'

'Cool,' Alfie says. 'So . . . what did you say you want for Christmas?'

I give him a sideways look. Alfie has dropped the madman-in-a-wind-tunnel look and his hair is almost normal now, slightly tousled and trimmed into a messy fringe. He has not been spotted lately in the school canteen throwing chips or juggling fruit or cramming whole puddings into his mouth sideways either, which has to be a big improvement.

One thing he will never be, though, is subtle.

'You're not really asking about me, are you?' I say with a sigh. 'You are asking about Summer. Admit it.'

Alfie goes pink. Really, it is very sad that he is crushing on someone who barely knows he exists. If my twin thinks about Alfie at all, it's probably in the way that you think about a small, annoying insect that is buzzing around you, just out of sight. You could swat that insect with a rolled-up newspaper and not think twice about it.

'What d'you think?' he asks, trying to be casual.

'She won't be expecting a present from you,' I say, as kindly as I can. 'It might not be a good idea.'

'I want to, though,' he frowns. 'I was going to leave it in her locker at school, with a card, but not actually sign it . . . that might get her thinking, right? And she'd know she has a secret admirer.'

'Maybe . . .'

'It's difficult, though,' he frowns. 'I was in town earlier, but I got really confused. What are you supposed to buy?

110

What do girls like? I thought a box of chocolates might be a bit of a cop-out in the circumstances . . .'

'It might,' I agree. 'Summer isn't easy to buy for. How about something practical? A nice warm pair of socks?'

'Are you kidding? You don't buy something practical for your girlfriend. Especially not socks!'

'I am kidding,' I grin. 'But, Alfie, she is not your girl-friend.'

'Not yet,' he says. 'I did get something in town. Shall I show you?'

The roundabout has spun to a standstill. Dusk falls around us like a blanket, muffling the sound of kids down on the high street, laughing and yelling, the rattle of a tractor up beyond the village. Alfie takes a small tissue-wrapped package from his pocket, unwrapping it carefully to reveal a pink silk rose attached to a shiny hairclip. It's beautiful – exactly the kind of thing Summer might pick out for herself.

'It's lovely,' I tell him. 'Perfect.'

Just like Summer herself, I think sourly, then feel instantly ashamed.

'You think so? Cool!' Alfie is saying. 'I appreciate it, you

❀❀❀❀❀❀❀❀❀❀❀❀❀❀❀❀❀❀❀❀

know – the advice about the hair and the messing around in class was top stuff. And I'm grateful that you haven't said anything to Summer. Um . . . you haven't, have you?'

'No, that bit's up to you.'

'Phew,' he grins. 'You're a good mate, Skye, I mean it. If there's ever anything I can do for you . . . well, y'know. Just ask.'

For a moment, I think about it. It would be good to talk to someone about all the stuff going round my head at the moment. But the things I want to say are too weird, too complicated. How can I tell Alfie I'm falling in love with a ghost boy? Or that Honey is on a collision course for disaster? Or that my twin sister is starting to feel like a stranger, these days . . .?

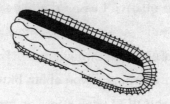

16

I say goodbye to Alfie and as I am walking home along the High Street, the bus pulls up ahead of me, a pool of yellow light in the darkness.

People get off, people with shopping bags and coat collars turned up against the cold, mums with pushchairs and toddlers, teenagers laughing and clowning around.

'Skye!' a voice calls out. 'Hang on! Wait for me!'

Summer is hurrying along the pavement towards me, her coat pulled tight against the cold.

'We were Christmas shopping,' Summer says, falling into step beside me, smiling as if we never fell out at all. 'Me and Tia. Well, window shopping in my case! I thought you were helping out in the workshop?'

'I was,' I say. 'I couldn't concentrate, so Paddy sent me

down to post some parcels . . . Summer – I feel rubbish. I hate it when we quarrel. I wish I'd never said anything to Honey.'

My twin hooks an arm through mine. 'Look . . . what I said earlier . . . snapping at you about how you spoke to Honey. I'm sorry, OK? I know you didn't mean anything. It's just . . . Honey seems so distant, so prickly, these days. I hate seeing her that way.'

'Me too,' I sigh. 'I get fed up treading on eggshells some-times, that's all.'

'I know,' Summer says. 'I hate it as well, but I always let her get away with it. For an easy life, I suppose – she's so mad at Mum and Paddy and Cherry, and I don't want her to be mad at me too. Does that make sense?'

'I guess,' I say. 'I don't want to lose her either, you know that. I just worry that the more we let her treat people that way, the worse she'll get.'

'You're probably right,' my twin sighs. 'I didn't mean to make you feel bad. I know you were only trying to help. It was just a surprise because usually you're trying to keep the peace, and lately . . . well, you're challenging Honey. Saying what you think.'

114

Is that Clara's influence, I wonder? I'm sure she must have been a girl who said what she thought.

'We can't let Honey go on thinking it's OK to act that way,' I sigh. 'Somebody has to say something, or she'll get worse and worse.'

'I guess,' Summer says. 'I just forget sometimes that you might have different ideas, different ways of handling things. Sorry, Skye.'

'It's OK.'

The idea that identical twins might not always have identical feelings and views is something I think Summer has always struggled with. But I'm not going to let that bother me now – we've cleared the air, wiped away the bad feeling. I'm relieved.

We walk along the lane for a while, and then Summer breaks the silence. 'Skye . . . I was just wondering . . . is everything OK with you and Millie?'

'Millie?' I echo. 'Yeah, I think so . . . Well, I guess she's kind of obsessed with boys and stuff lately. I'm trying not to get wound up by it.'

'It's just . . . something funny happened today, Skye. Millie was chatting with me and Tia one lunchtime – I think you

❀❀❀❀❀❀❀❀❀❀❀❀❀❀❀❀❀❀❀❀❀

were at Drama Club – and she heard us talking about going shopping today. I think she was angling for an invite too, but I didn't suss it at the time.'

'Oh, she's got this thing about us all hanging out at that new cafe on the Esplanade in town,' I explain. 'Loads of kids from the high school go there, apparently, and she thinks she might get chatted up. I said I was busy, but it's not my kind of thing anyway, Millie knows that.'

'OK,' Summer says. 'It's just . . . well, she turned up today. We didn't ask her along, honest, but she tracked us down and latched on, as if we'd all been planning to meet. And she did drag us to the cafe, but it was full of mums and toddlers and it was so expensive we had to have one cappuccino between three. Nobody was chatted up, that's for sure. It was all a bit weird!'

There's a little jolt of hurt inside me. For years now, it has always been Summer and Tia, Millie and me. Sometimes we all hang out together, and there's actually no reason why Millie shouldn't spend some time with Summer and Tia, but . . . why didn't she mention it to me?

Millie has always liked Summer, but in a sweet, star-struck way, as if my twin was slightly out of her league. They're

❀ ❀ ❀ ❀ ❀ ❀ ❀ ❀ ❀ ❀ ❀ ❀ ❀ ❀ ❀ ❀ ❀ ❀ ❀ ❀

not friends in the way we're friends – Millie and I under-stand each other, we've always been close.

Suddenly, it's starting to look a little different. Did Millie want to hang out with Summer all along? Am I second best to my own twin – again?

'Maybe she was in town anyway,' I say, looking for an excuse so it won't seem like my best friend is ditching me.

'Maybe,' Summer agrees. 'I just thought I'd say. She is hanging around me and Tia a lot these days. It's weird, and it was weird it being the three of us today, without you.'

Summer and I don't say any more about it, but I am starting to feel more and more like a shadow girl. First Alfie, then Millie, both crushing on my twin in their own ways. Why does nothing ever seem to be truly mine?

Predictably, Honey doesn't appear at supper. We eat the cream cakes, but the rich, sweet taste can't take away the sourness from the day.

Before I go to bed I leave the cake box with Honey's lone chocolate eclair just outside the door of the turret bedroom, a peace offering, and in the morning, sure enough, it's gone.

17

The following weekend we go to pick up the Christmas tree. It may not be the tallest one in Somerset, but it's big all right. It takes all of us to lift it off the roof of Paddy's mini-van and carry it into the house, hauling it upright in a slow battle with spiky branches running their fingers through our hair.

Honey is the only one not helping, but at least she is still speaking to me, thank goodness. She used to love putting up the Christmas tree, when we were younger, but these days everyone knows it'll be way less stressful without her.

'It's the best tree we've ever had!' I declare.

'We might need more tinsel,' Summer says.

'And another string of lights,' Coco says, deflated. 'We'll have to wait to decorate it. I wanted to do it now!'

❀❀❀❀❀❀❀❀❀❀❀❀❀❀❀❀❀❀❀❀❀❀

'We can,' Paddy says brightly. 'We've got our stuff from the Glasgow flat! There's plenty of tinsel, and baubles, and another string of lights. Cherry, I think our box of decorations is in the storeroom next to the workshop . . .'

'Ours is on top of my wardrobe if someone wants to fetch it,' Mum says. 'And then I think we need the Christmas CD . . .'

We take our time with the decorations, listening to cheesy Christmas songs and draping coloured lights and shiny baubles and the brightly painted wooden decorations that belong to Paddy and Cherry in among the branches. We add the home-made decorations too, the lumpy salt-dough shapes we made when we were little, the sequinned felt hearts, the little criss-crossy twig stars sprayed with fake snow.

There are even six beautiful birds, made from glittery card with carefully folded paper tails that look like Japanese fans, Cherry's origami-inspired contribution.

Mixing two boxes of decorations together feels good, like combining our two families to make one patched-together one. It's like adding 2 + 2 and coming up with a whole lot more than 4, if that makes sense.

'Which angel?' Mum asks as we look at the two contenders, the Costellos' cool sparkly shop-bought one and our papier-mâché ballerina, dressed in vintage silk and net. We've had it forever – Mum made it herself, back in her art student days, and I have always loved it.

'It has to be your ballerina one,' Cherry says firmly. 'It's gorgeous.'

Paddy lifts Coco up to place the ballerina angel on the top of the tree and Summer switches the lights on and we cheer. The tree looks magical, like something from a storybook.

'It smells so good,' I breathe. 'Like Christmas!'

'We're doing it properly this year,' Mum grins. 'Our way. New traditions to suit ourselves, mix it up a bit, make it special!'

'Will we still hang up stockings?' Coco wants to know. 'I know we are practically teenagers now, but we have to have stockings.'

'Me and Skye will be thirteen in February,' Summer points out. 'You are only eleven, Coco. You're miles behind us.'

'But we're definitely not too old for stockings,' I put in. 'Any of us. Along the mantlepiece?'

❀❀❀❀❀❀❀❀❀❀❀❀❀❀❀❀❀❀❀❀❀

'I used to have a pillowcase at the end of the bed,' Cherry says. 'But stockings along the mantlepiece would be cool!'

'We always write lists for Santa and throw them into the fire and see if the wind takes them up the chimney,' Coco says. 'Can we still do that?'

'Can we have yule log instead of Christmas pudding?' I request.

'And no sprouts?' Paddy chips in.

'And nut roast instead of turkey because I am vegetarian?' Coco adds.

'Anything you want,' Mum laughs. 'Nut roast is fine, but the rest of us might still want turkey, Coco! And I'd quite like a Christmas Eve party, invite some of the friends and neighbours. Fancy it?'

'Cool!' Summer says. 'And you'll all come and see me in the dance-school Christmas show, won't you?'

'Wow – yes please,' Cherry says. 'I've never been to a ballet before!'

On Friday, Summer discovers Alfie's card and present in her locker. (The lockers at Exmoor Park Middle School never actually lock – we lost the keys so often Mr King got all stressed out and did away with them completely.)

'Who could it be?' she asks, wide-eyed. 'It's beautiful! But it just says *a secret admirer*, so I have absolutely no idea . . .'

She shows me the card, which features a ballerina girl wearing a Santa hat and a red dress trimmed with white fun fur. I spot Alfie across the corridor, watching, his lips twitching into a smile as Summer slides the pink flower hairclip into her hair.

'Wow,' Millie breathes at my elbow. 'This is so, so romantic!'

'Could it be Aaron Jones?' Summer muses. 'He's in my French class. Or Carl Watson? Or Sid Sharma?'

'Or someone else completely,' I say carefully, trying not to catch Alfie's eye.

'Shall I ask Aaron?' Millie offers. 'Go on, Summer, I don't mind. You need to know, and I will be very subtle.'

'No, it's OK, Millie,' Summer says, and that's a good call, because Millie is about as subtle as a leopard-skin bikini. 'Aaron's cute, though. Tia's always saying she thinks he might fancy me. But then, Carl did wink at me yesterday in the dinner hall, and lots of girls are crushing on Carl.

Then again, Sid's little sister does ballet, so I see him at the dance school sometimes, and he is SO much nicer out of school.'

'Summer,' I say. 'I thought you weren't interested in boys?'

'I'm not,' she shrugs. 'Just . . . curious, y'know! You would be too, if it was you!'

'It's not me, though, is it?' I say, and somehow it comes out kind of sad and mean, so I laugh to take the sting out of my words.

'It will be,' Summer grins. 'Soon, I bet. I can't explain, Skye, it makes you feel all tingly and happy inside to know that somebody . . . well, y'know. Likes you.'

'Don't worry,' Millie chips in. 'We grow up at our own pace, all the magazines say so. I expect you'll catch up soon, Skye!'

I try to smile, but a fizz of anger simmers inside me. I feel much older and wiser than Millie, sometimes. Growing up is not all about glittery lipgloss and clumpy shoes and dissolving into giggles whenever a boy looks in your direction, surely? But Millie's words make me feel about five years old.

❀❀❀❀❀❀❀❀❀❀❀❀❀❀❀❀❀❀

As for Summer – well, I do know about the tingly, happy feeling she's talking about, even if it is only from my dreams.

All week the dreams have been running through my sleep like an old movie, a Technicolor window on someone else's past. And ever since Mrs Lee's weird prediction last week, thoughts of Finch are refusing to stay confined to dreams. They seep out into the daytime too.

It's like having a secret crush, but one who is even more unattainable than a movie star or an indie-band boy. I don't believe in ghosts, so how come I am crushing on one?

'What if the present isn't from Aaron or Carl or Sid?' I ask my twin. 'What if it's someone ordinary? Or . . . someone annoying?'

Summer frowns. 'Well, it won't be, will it?' she says, puzzled. 'It's definitely someone cool. You can tell because of the thought that's gone into it.'

'Right . . .'

'Someone like . . . well, like Alfie Anderson, for example, would never think of this,' she says. 'If he was trying to impress someone, he'd give them chewing gum that made their tongue go blue, or a stink bomb or something.'

✿✿✿✿✿✿✿✿✿✿✿✿✿✿✿✿✿✿✿✿✿

In the distance I see Alfie gazing over, starry-eyed. Some-times, ignorance really is bliss.

'Let's meet at lunchtime,' Millie is saying to my twin. 'We can make a list of possible boys. And then we could start chatting to them, all casual, and see if they seem interested . . . oh, this is so exciting!'

The bell rings and Summer heads off to class, Millie cling-ing on to her arm. I am torn between hurt for Alfie, hurt that no one would think to send *me* a Christmas love note, and hurt that my best friend is drifting away from me.

These last few weeks, Millie doesn't want to talk about hopes, dreams or ambitions. She doesn't want to talk about the chocolate workshop or going to the beach or what it would be like to go back in history and wear a crinoline dress and style your hair in ringlets. She only wants to talk about boys.

Well, that's fine – I guess. I just never thought she'd ditch me for my twin sister.

We are walking through the woods, dappled sunlight filtering through the trees, the skinny lurcher dog running on ahead over the soft, mossy ground, the blush-pink mallow flowers to either side of us.

It's hot, even in the soft shade of the woods. Finch holds my hand in his, and even though I cannot hear what he is saying, I can feel the warmth of his skin against mine. He is grinning, talking, brushing the dark waves back from his face, pulling the red neckerchief loose as he pulls me forward through the little twisty trees.

When we reach the stile at the edge of the woods, he jumps over quickly, turning back to help me climb it. He's in a white shirt and red braces, his waistcoat unbuttoned, sleeves rolled up, his bare arms tanned as he reaches up to lift me down.

I spin away from him, running down through a meadow starred with wildflowers. I splash through a stream, run on through another field, face turned up to the blue sky, laughing.

We're at the beach, and he takes my hand again, helping me over the rocks, and we slip and slide across the stones and shells and the gritty sand until we're at the ocean's edge, the cold water rushing against our feet.

And then his arms fold round me, holding me close, so close I can hear his heartbeat. When his lips touch mine I don't know who I am any more, Skye Tanberry or Clara Travers or someone else completely, and I don't even care. I just care about the taste of salt and happiness, my fingers sliding down his cheek, twining into his hair. The warm sun beats down on us, the icy water laps our feet, and I have never felt so alive, alive, alive.

*

It is just a dream, of course, but when I wake I can still taste salt. Perhaps it's just my tears? It's not real, and I want it to be, so, so much. I turn over and close my eyes, but I cannot get back to the dream, no matter how hard I try.

18

The next Saturday, Cherry moves into her new bedroom. Mum and Summer have gone into town, for ballet-lesson and Christmas-shopping purposes respectively, and Coco is out in the workshop, helping Paddy with the chocolate orders, which are coming in faster than ever.

I make two mugs of steaming hot chocolate heaped with marshmallows and climb the little wooden ladder that leads up from our landing into the new attic bedroom, sticking my head through the hatch.

'Hey!' Cherry grins. 'Skye! Come on up!'

Mum and Paddy have painted the walls pale yellow and put together an old iron bedstead they found in the attic space, with a new mattress and a feather duvet and the patchwork quilt from the caravan. There's a stripy rag rug

❀❀❀❀❀❀❀❀❀❀❀❀❀❀❀❀❀❀❀❀❀

on the sanded floorboards, a pine dressing table and a clothes rail Paddy has made himself from a length of broomstick.

The little attic windows are hung with Japanese *noren* door curtains with a geisha print, a parasol is suspended from the ceiling to serve as a lampshade and Cherry's cool kimono is pinned to one wall. It looks awesome, and neat and tidy too, the kind of bedroom where you would never lose a bundle of hundred-year-old letters.

'This room is the best!' Cherry says, arranging her clothes on the broomstick rail and folding her socks and tights into a drawer. 'It's about a million miles away from my old room in Glasgow, I swear. I love the sloping walls and the little windows – if you stand right on tiptoes there's actually a view of the sea in the distance!'

I set down the drinks and sink on to a floor cushion. 'Fancy a hot chocolate break?'

'Too right,' Cherry grins, flopping down on to the bed. 'How's stuff with you then, Skye?'

'Great,' I say. 'Well . . . mostly great.'

'OK . . . so which bits aren't?'

Where do I start? I can talk to my stepsister about most

things, but I'm not sure a crush on a long-dead gypsy boy is the kind of thing she'll understand. I'd like to tell her about the dreams, but wouldn't she think I was crazy?

I dig up something a little less unsettling to share.

'Growing up is such a pain,' I sigh. 'Millie's gone all weird, pretty much overnight – she's so hung up on boys and make-up now. She treats me as if I'm some little kid these days.'

'Sounds like she's trying too hard,' Cherry says. 'D'you think she's feeling a bit out of her depth?'

I frown. 'Maybe. I don't know – Millie has always jumped from one mad craze to another, but this one is really bugging me. Maybe I'm the one feeling out of my depth? This whole growing-up thing still feels kind of scary to me.'

'You're doing fine,' Cherry says. 'It's not all about boys and make-up and short skirts – Millie will work that out sooner or later.'

'I hope so,' I sigh. 'But it feels like we're drifting apart, like she'd rather be with Summer. I mean, I can't exactly blame her . . .'

There's a sparkle about Summer, a shine, something that

attracts people and keeps them close, fluttering about her like moths round a flame. But does she really need another for her collection? Does she really need Millie?

'Millie met up with Summer and Tia in town last weekend,' I sigh. 'She hasn't even mentioned it . . . I only know because Summer told me. What if I'm losing her, Cherry? What if she's bored with me?'

'Trust me, nobody could ever be bored with you, Skye,' Cherry says. 'You're one of the coolest people I know. But . . . well, you've been a bit distant, distracted, lately. Like you're off in your own world the whole time. Maybe that's the problem?'

I frown. Is it wrong to want to hide away in the past when the present is so uncertain, the future scary? I don't think so.

'Millie needs you,' Cherry shrugs. 'That whole town thing might have been a way of getting your attention, making you feel jealous even. Don't throw a whole friendship away just because one of you is changing a bit. Work at it. I know what I'm talking about, Skye – I didn't have any real friends until I came here, so I know how important it is. Don't give up on Millie!'

❀❀❀❀❀❀❀❀❀❀❀❀❀❀❀❀❀❀❀❀❀

I am not planning to give up on Millie, but sometimes I worry that she is giving up on me. I push the thought away, firmly.

'Anyway,' my stepsister grins. 'You know where I am if you need to talk. I'm going to miss huddling into the caravan, though, even if it is a *lot* warmer in here!'

'We can still use it as a meeting place, can't we?' I say, sipping the last of my hot chocolate.

'Definitely,' Cherry agrees. 'Did you hear that Dad is going to paint up the caravan in time for the wedding? Charlotte wants to borrow a horse from the farm and drive it down to Kitnor Church instead of a wedding car!'

My eyes widen. 'That would be so cool!' I breathe. 'We did take it down to the village once, years ago, for the Kitnor Food Fair.'

I lean back against the bed. A picture flashes into my mind, of our caravan, the same but different, crowded together with the others from my dream, down in the woods. Is it a dream, or an imagining, or a shadow from the past?

Clara's letters have well and truly vanished, so I'll probably never know.

❀❀❀❀❀❀❀❀❀❀❀❀❀❀❀❀❀❀❀❀❀❀❀

'Do you believe in ghosts?' I ask suddenly, and Cherry looks up, startled.

'Ghosts?' she echoes.

'Well, you know. Spirits from the past,' I say, my cheeks pink. 'Reaching out to the present somehow . . .' I wasn't going to talk about this, but Cherry's a good listener, and how else am I going to puzzle out what the dreams mean?

A shadow crosses Cherry's face. 'No, I don't believe in ghosts. If they existed, I think my mum would have found a way to reach me.'

I bite my lip. Stupid, stupid, stupid.

'Oh, Cherry, I'm sorry! I shouldn't have said anything.'

She sighs. 'It's OK. All that was a long time ago. I've accepted it now. But . . . funny question, Skye! Has something happened?'

'Not really,' I say. 'It's just that story about Clara, the gypsies . . . I can't get it out of my head. Finding the trunk of clothes – well, it's made it all seem so real.'

Cherry is listening carefully, and I wonder why I can tell her this when I can't, daren't, mention it to Summer. Is it because Summer would be frightened, furious? She'd probably make a bonfire of the dresses, so I'd have no link left with Clara, with Finch. I can't risk that. Or is it just that lately Summer and I seem to be drifting further and further apart?

I take a deep breath. 'You said I seemed a bit distant, dreamy, lately . . . well, you're probably right. I've been having these strange dreams, like snapshots of the past, fragments of memory . . . about the gypsies in the woods. It has to be linked with Clara, doesn't it?'

Cherry considers. 'It could just be your imagination,' she says. 'It's such a sad story, and finding the trunk like that – perhaps your unconscious is filling in the details a little, trying to find a happy ending?'

I shrug. 'It's just – well, it feels like more than that. It feels as if I can't let go, can't step back.'

'They're dreams, though,' Cherry says reasonably. 'That's not the same as actually seeing ghosts, is it?'

'No . . . so, you don't think there's a reason for it then?' I ask. 'It's not some kind of mystery I have to unravel? You know, like in those spooky movies you see where some ghost is lingering on because they want people to discover the truth about what really happened in the past? Because it feels a bit like that, sometimes.'

❀❀❀❀❀❀❀❀❀❀❀❀❀❀❀❀❀❀❀❀❀❀

Cherry's eyes are wide, concerned. 'God, Skye . . . you think Clara's trying to tell you something? Like . . . maybe she didn't kill herself after all? Maybe she was . . . murdered? Scary!'

I shake my head. 'No, I don't think it's anything like that. It's not scary at all. I can't explain. It doesn't feel frightening or sinister, but . . . there must be something, surely? Some reason I can't let go of it?'

Cherry looks troubled. 'Clara's story has really hit home for you,' she says. 'I can see that. But you can't let it take over. Nobody's trying to tell you stuff, and there is no mystery, you know that.'

'Ignore me, I'm just being silly.' I laugh, trying to lighten the mood. I don't want Cherry to think I'm really losing it. 'You're right, I've let my imagination run away with me. Thanks for listening, Cherry – it doesn't seem such a big deal any more. Just a couple of weird dreams.'

She nods and we let the subject go. There may be no such thing as ghosts, but as Mrs Lee said, there could be a whole lot of things out there we don't yet understand.

All I know is that a boy called Finch has lodged himself inside my head, my heart – and I don't want to let him go.

My stepsister is arranging stuff on her dressing table –

hairbrush, make-up, bodyspray and bracelets. She takes out a little photo of Shay and clips it to the side of the mirror, where she can see it every day.

'Did you know, right from the start, with Shay?' I ask. 'That you liked him?'

Cherry rolls her eyes. 'No way. I thought he was vain and arrogant and annoying. I thought Honey was welcome to him.'

'What changed?' I ask, curious now.

'I got to know him,' she sighs. 'I tried and tried not to fall for him, Skye. I knew he was off-limits, but I couldn't help it. I just couldn't.'

'Do you love him?' I dare to ask.

Cherry's cheeks flush pink. 'I think so. I think I do.'

'But . . . how do you know?' I ask. 'I mean . . . what does it feel like?'

Cherry shrugs. 'I think about him all the time. I want to be with him. My heart races and the breath catches in my throat . . .'

She looks at me carefully. 'Skye? Is there someone you like too?'

It's my turn to blush. 'There might be . . .'

❀❀❀❀❀❀❀❀❀❀❀❀❀❀❀❀❀❀❀❀❀

'That Alfie boy from Halloween? The one Summer's been teasing you about?' Cherry wants to know.

I laugh. 'No, no, not Alfie. Definitely not Alfie . . . It's complicated.' I tell her.

Cherry smiles sadly.

'It's always complicated,' she says.

19

We make our Christmas wish lists on little squares of coloured tissue paper, neatly writing down the things we'd like most in the world. It's easy for Coco, who writes *a pony* in block capitals and then *riding lessons*; *a llama*; *a donkey*; *a parrot*. Cherry asks for things for her new room, like fairy lights and posters, and Summer asks for pointe shoes, which I know she has wanted forever and can finally actually use.

I find it harder to decide because the things I want are not actually things I can have. I have always felt this way, ever since the year Dad left and I realized I couldn't write his name at the top of my Christmas list in case it upset Mum. So what do I want this year? To wear the velvet dresses from Clara's trunk, to dream of Finch, to step back in time and kiss him on the lips and see if it feels as good as when I dreamt it? I'm not sure Santa could sort that one.

I remember a gypsy-style shawl I spotted in a shop in Minehead, and write that down instead.

The others are still writing, but I abandon my list and raid the kitchen for supplies so that I can make marshmallow s'mores on the open fire. I warm marshmallows on the old toasting fork until they are golden, then sandwich them quickly between two chocolate digestives so that the marshmallow and the chocolate melt together in one perfect, soft-sweet smudge of biscuit and mallow fluff. Coco and Cherry pounce on them, but Summer wrinkles up her nose.

'Must be about a million calories in those,' she says. 'Yuck.'

I stick my tongue out at her and bite into my s'more. Who cares about the calories when it tastes so good anyway?

Mum comes in with a couple of logs for the fire, which is probably just a sneaky way of taking a look at our wish lists.

'That's a very small list,' she says when she sees mine. 'Stuck for ideas?'

'I don't know what I want,' I shrug, although that's not

strictly true. 'Something vintage, something cool. I don't know. A surprise, I guess.'

'Fair enough,' Mum says.

I pick up my list, still trying to make the marshmallow sweetness last, and in the corner of the paper, I draw a picture of a little bird, small and neat with a gently forking tail, an image that has started appearing all over my notebooks lately, all over my heart.

'What's that?' Coco wants to know. 'Are you asking for a budgie or something?'

'Just doodling,' I say.

'It could be a little bird, to go in the birdcage in our room,' Summer says, flinging herself down on the carpet beside me.

'I don't like birds in cages, Summer, you know that.'

'I know,' my twin says. 'I had a brilliant idea, though – we could ask for a birthday party, a special, grown-up one for our thirteenth. What do you think?'

What do I think? Cake and hot chocolate in the Mad Hatter would suit me way better than some awkward teen party where the girls dress up in too-smart clothes and totter around sipping Coke and eyeing up a handful of spotty,

❀❀❀❀❀❀❀❀❀❀❀❀❀❀❀❀❀❀❀❀

oafish lads. I think it sounds like torture, but Summer clearly doesn't.

I consider smiling and going along with my twin, but when I look back, I can remember going along with a whole lot of things that Summer thought would be cool. There was never much time to spare for the stuff I wanted to do. I don't want to do that any more.

'I'm not sure if that's my kind of thing, Summer,' I say gently. 'I'm not really a party girl.'

'I'm writing it down,' she says. 'Perfect prezzie, really, because it's for both of us . . . we could have a Valentine's Day theme!'

I wonder when Summer stopped listening to me, stopped thinking about the things I wanted? A while ago, I think.

'It's a lovely idea,' Mum says, moving the fireguard aside. 'But parties are a little tricky these days, now that we have the B&B . . .'

'Well, I can wish,' Summer says, grinning. 'We've got nothing to lose, right?' She walks over to the fire and throws her list into the flames, and the rest of us follow. According to the family tradition, if the draught catches them and pulls them up the chimney, we'll get what we have asked for. If they fall into the fire, we won't. Summer's list flies up the chimney, then Coco's and Cherry's.

Mine falls into the flames and is consumed in a puff of blue smoke. Typical.

The foyer of the Exmoor Royal Theatre is crammed with families, all dressed up in their Christmas best, buying programmes and sipping drinks and talking about the show. Earlier, when we dropped Summer backstage, the place was even crazier . . . little girls running around in elf or fairy or bluebird costumes, their lips scarlet, their cheeks dusted with glitter, hair scraped up into perfect buns; helpers pinning costumes and wiping tears and finding lost shoes; teachers counting children, checking lists, yelling instructions.

I remember it all, the buzz of excitement, the ache of anxiety, the fug of hairspray and hysteria mixed in together. Summer and I would dress and have our hair checked and our make-up done, then check the clock on the wall in the junior dressing room a million times as we waited for our class to be called onstage.

It was often a long wait, so we'd eat the sandwiches Mum

made for us and read comics and do puzzles with the other girls, talking about how cool it would be if we were waiting for our curtain call at Sadler's Wells or Covent Garden Opera House: famous, fabulous, our photographs framed on the dressing-room walls.

I wonder if Summer still remembers that?

This year the show is *Cinderella*. After the interval, Summer is dancing in the ballroom scenes with the senior classes. I've seen her costume, and it's stunning, a calf-length tutu of pale blue net and chiffon, like a wisp of cloud. She has a silver tiara for her hair and a little blue fan, which is part of the dance.

Before all that, in the first half of the show, she is a student helper for the pre-primary class, who are dressed as bluebirds and just have to flap their wings and point their toes and skip about a bit – Summer's job is to lead them on to the stage, holding hands with the littlest bluebird, and do the steps alongside them so that nobody forgets.

'It's exciting!' Cherry says, sipping Coke and looking around her. 'I've never actually been to a proper theatre before!'

'My fault,' Paddy admits. 'We used to do the multiplex

✿✿✿✿✿✿✿✿✿✿✿✿✿✿✿✿✿✿✿✿✿✿✿

cinema once in a while, but theatres and ballet . . . well, I never really thought of it. And we know the prima ballerina too!'

'She isn't actually the prima ballerina,' Coco points out.

'She will be, one day,' Paddy says. 'And she's a star to me!'

The only person not here is Honey, who said she has sat through enough ballet-school shows to last her a lifetime.

'Are you really not coming?' I asked her, earlier, and Honey shrugged. 'I can't,' she said. 'Not with Paddy and Cherry there, Skye. Seriously. I'm sorry.'

'Tell that to Summer,' I said, and in the end Honey came with us to the theatre after all, hugging Summer and telling her she'd be brilliant before heading off to town to meet her friends.

We make our way up to the dress circle, find our seats and settle in, flicking through the programme, and slowly the seats around us fill up. Cherry is still scanning the auditorium, taking in the heavy crimson curtains and the gold trim and the old-fashioned seats when suddenly the music stills and the lights are dimmed.

The shows always follow the same kind of formula; the dance school takes a story and choreographs something

❀❀❀❀❀❀❀❀❀❀❀❀❀❀❀❀❀❀❀❀❀❀❀

that follows it loosely, using it as a vehicle for every class to have their moment in the spotlight. Cinderella is a girl from the Intermediate class, the one Summer is joining in January, and the stepsisters are played by two brave girls who don't mind the garish make-up, hideous wigs and nasty nylon dresses. The prince, according to Summer, has been imported from a dance school in Exeter because there are no boy dancers the right age at her school. The wicked stepmother is played by a man in drag, a friend of Miss Elise's who works in the theatre for a living, and he narrates the show and throws a few jokes in to link things together with a bit of a pantomime flavour.

When Summer comes onstage holding one of the little bluebird girls by the hand, I am so proud I could burst. She moves so easily across the stage, willowy and elegant in her bluebird costume, while the little ones look up at her in awe.

I know how they feel.

I look at the children and spot a girl in the back row who reminds me of the way I used to be, distracted and looking in the wrong direction, too busy fiddling with her feathery cap to flap her arms in time with the music. Then the dance is over and Summer is leading them away, and the little girl

I was watching trips and panics and starts to cry . . . my twin runs back and scoops her up and carries her offstage, and the audience coo and clap and cheer.

I smile for the little girl I used to be, and for the way Summer always looked out for me, holding my hand, picking me up when I fell down. That was the plus side of being a twin, and I miss that closeness. It's like it's slipped away – so slowly I didn't really notice.

Later, Summer's class comes on, each girl dressed in sugar-candy shades for the ballroom scenes. I remember some of these girls, of course. I wasn't the only one to drop out along the way, but I realize now that not everyone who stayed is naturally talented. Some of them are too stiff, too slow, too awkward. It doesn't seem to bother them, though, as they swirl around the stage, chins tilted, arms curved into the softest of curves as they move on tiptoe. Perhaps ballet is something I might have stuck with if it hadn't meant being so very much in my sister's shadow.

Summer is definitely the best dancer in the group. She even has a short solo, spinning round with the prince in her cloudy-blue tutu, twirling and leaping as if the music has hold of her, as if it's in her soul.

❀❀❀❀❀❀❀❀❀❀❀❀❀❀❀❀❀❀❀❀❀❀❀

'Wow, wow, WOW,' Cherry whispers as the dance ends and the audience whistle and cheer. 'She's AWESOME! Really!'

'I know,' I grin, but I think I am realizing it for the first time. Summer is talented, really talented at dance. We all know how the *Cinderella* story ends, but trust me, that prince would have been crazy not to choose my sister.

20

The house smells of pine needles, warm mince pies and the rich, spicy aroma of mulled wine. The walls are draped with strings of Christmas cards, brightly wrapped presents lie piled up beneath the tree and sprigs of holly and ivy are tucked behind every picture.

In the kitchen, the table is heaped with buffet food – warm sausage rolls, quiche and every kind of sweet treat, from sherry trifle and Christmas cake to a mountain of profiteroles. All around the house, jam-jar lanterns and candles flicker, and a huge tangle of mistletoe and ribbon hangs from the lampshade in the living room. Mum and Paddy have already insisted on using it, which was kind of icky, but then again they are getting married in the summer so it is probably allowed.

The CD player is pelting out Christmas songs and even the weather is trying to play along, because it's positively arctic, and a thick frost has brushed everything outside with a shimmer of white that sparkles in the fading light.

The B&B is closed until after New Year, so the guest lounge and the breakfast room are opened up for us to use, and I think we are going to need them because the first few party guests have started to arrive and already the place is filling up.

Mum seems to have asked almost everyone. Millie is here with her mum and dad, and Joe the farmer who brought in his digger to help to make the goldfish pond for us back in the summer is here with his family, and there's a whole bunch of Mum and Paddy's friends from the village.

Summer, Cherry, Coco and I have tinsel in our hair as we hand out drinks and sausage rolls. Honey is wearing a fluffy jumper and shorts that are so tiny you could be forgiven for mistaking her blue opaque tights for a severe case of frostbite. She has neatly opted out of the tinsel and the helping out in favour of flirting with Joe-the-farmer's teenage son.

The doorbell rings and I run off to answer it. There on

the doorstep are Alfie Anderson, his cute, jumble-sale-bright little sisters and his hippy-dippy mum and dad, so I show them in and ply them with mulled wine and warm cranberry punch.

'Need a hand?' Alfie asks, appearing at my elbow as I load up a tray with sausage rolls and mini quiche. 'I can make myself useful.'

'Erm – maybe make yourself scarce, instead?' Summer says, ladling cranberry punch into paper cups.

'I like that flower thing in your hair,' Alfie tells her brightly, eyeing up the pink flower hairclip that's pinning her tinsel headband in place. 'Where did you get it?'

'From a friend,' Summer says, elbowing past him with the drinks tray. 'A close friend.'

Alfie's grin is so big it lights up his whole face, but Summer has long gone. 'Did you hear that?' he asks, snaffling a sausage roll. 'A close friend! Summer sees me as a close friend!'

'Alfie,' I sigh. 'She thinks someone else sent it. Don't get your hopes up. She made a list of possible admirers, and you weren't even on it.'

'I know, but she will work it out eventually,' he insists.

❀❀❀❀❀❀❀❀❀❀❀❀❀❀❀❀❀❀❀❀❀❀❀

'And she will notice me. I've changed. And the changes are an improvement, right?'

'Definitely,' I say, slapping his hand as he reaches for another sausage roll. 'And you are determined, I will say that for you.'

'You've been brilliant, Skye,' he says, following me back out into the party scrum. 'I am learning a lot from you. Pretty soon, I will be irresistible to women, yeah?'

'Let's not get carried away,' I say, smiling sweetly as I try to navigate through the crush. 'One step at a time. There is someone for everybody in this world, Alfie, I am just not sure if Summer is the one for you.'

'She is,' he tells me confidently. 'She just doesn't know it yet. And tonight could be the night. I'm not straying far from this mistletoe, OK?'

There can be a very fine line between determination and stupidity, and I think that Alfie Anderson has just crossed it, but I am much too polite to say so. I shrug and smile and hand him one last sausage roll, then leave him to it.

Two hours later, the crowd has dwindled. I have eaten too many mince pies and danced to way too many cheesy Christmas songs and I am now officially partied-out. The living room has been taken over by tipsy adults talking about politics and the scandalous cost of Christmas. The remaining teens and pre-teens are flaked out in the breakfast room playing Truth or Dare, and a few little kids are ransacking what's left of the cake and racing around the place on a wild sugar high.

Carrying a handful of empty glasses back to the kitchen, I pass Paddy talking to Joe the farmer in the hallway about the best diet for orphan lambs. A little further on I spot Fred the dog eating a stash of stolen sausage rolls behind the sofa and Honey kissing Joe-the-farmer's son on the stairs. I am guessing this means the Year Twelve boyfriend is history now.

I dump the glasses next to the sink, grab a random jacket from the rack and head out into the darkness, crunching across the frost-white grass to the gypsy caravan. It looks just like the one in my dreams, and right now that dream world is where I'd rather be, so I just about jump out of my skin when I see a hunched figure sitting on the caravan steps.

This is not dream territory, though, trust me.

'Alfie,' I sigh. 'What are you doing here?'

'Keeping a lookout for flying reindeer,' he says, deadpan. 'How about you?'

'Same, obviously,' I reply, sitting down beside him. 'The party's winding down. No luck with the mistletoe?'

'Nah,' he says. 'I am invisible. I stood there so long a bit of the stuff dropped off, and I took it over to where Summer was standing and waved it in the air . . . she told me to get lost.'

'OK. That's probably a no, then . . .'

Alfie fishes the sprig of mistletoe from his pocket. 'Can't interest you, Skye, can I? Might be a cool way of keeping warm!'

I jump back, horrified.

'Me?' I squeak. 'That's not funny, Alfie. Summer and I may be identical twins, but we are very different people. You can't kiss me instead of her just because it's dark and we look alike!'

'OK, OK, just asking!'

'You fancy Summer, not me!' I argue. 'It would be wrong, Alfie, in all kinds of ways. Let's just say that whole irresistible-to-women thing hasn't quite kicked in yet.'

'Worth a try,' he sighs, chucking down the mistletoe. 'I

wasn't trying to be funny. It's just . . . well, I'm alone and you're alone, and I have never actually kissed a girl before, so . . . I thought it could be another life lesson, maybe – like the stuff about the hair and the practical jokes and not stuffing 103 sausage rolls into my mouth at the same time. We could help each other.'

'My life lessons don't extend to kissing practice,' I say sternly.

What is it with boys? Alfie still has a whole lot to learn if he thinks I am about to be his Christmas Eve consolation prize. Why am I always, somehow, second best to Summer, destined to pick up her cast-offs? When we were little, it was toys and dolls and ballet books she'd finished with; these days it is nail varnish and blue fringey scarves and boys.

Finch, at least, is nobody's cast-off. He is mine alone, even if he does exist only in my dreams.

'I still love Summer,' Alfie is insisting. 'She is definitely the only girl for me. It's just that sometimes I get disheartened. I wonder if I'm fooling myself . . . if it's all completely hopeless. You'll understand one day, Skye, when you fall for someone.'

I grit my teeth, exasperated.

❀❀❀❀❀❀❀❀❀❀❀❀❀❀❀❀❀❀❀❀❀❀

'Who says I haven't?'

Alfie gawps at me in the moonlight. 'You're crushing on someone? Who is it? Tell me!'

'I can't tell you,' I say. 'It's nobody you know. And it's all completely pointless because I can't have him anyway. If you think your situation is hopeless, forget it. Mine is downright impossible.'

'Oh, man,' Alfie marvels. 'I am guessing it must be someone a good bit older than you, if he is so out-of-reach and impossible. Am I right?'

'No, I think he's my age,' I say. 'Maybe a year older at most. It's not that simple, Alfie, trust me . . .'

I trail away into silence, frowning. Something's not right, but I can't work out why. Over the last few weeks, even without the proof the missing letters might provide, I've pretty much convinced myself that Finch is a ghost boy, that I am dreaming fragments of memory from Clara's life. I don't know why – maybe I am a little bit psychic, like Mrs Lee has always said, and I'm picking up faint memories of the past from Clara's velvet dresses, her locket, her bracelets?

But if Clara Travers fell in love with a gypsy boy, he must have been at least seventeen, like she was. Maybe older.

❀❀❀❀❀❀❀❀❀❀❀❀❀❀❀❀❀❀❀❀❀

Definitely not thirteen or fourteen, or whatever the boy in my dreams seems to be.

This means Finch can't be the ghost of a long-dead gypsy boy . . . he must be made-up.

I know it doesn't make any difference whether he once existed or not. I know the facts are the same; I can never meet him, not outside my dreams. But even so, a little stab of sadness twists inside me at the thought that Finch was never real, never as alive as he appears to me.

I sigh in the darkness, and Alfie sighs with me.

21

'Wake up, Skye!' Coco yells, dragging my duvet off. 'Summer, wake up! It's Christmas!'

'It's still dark!'

'It's half eight!' Coco insists. 'We have never slept so late on Christmas Day before! Come ON!'

'I've been awake for hours,' Cherry says from the doorway. 'I'm so excited . . . my first Christmas at Tanglewood!'

Coco runs off to wake Honey, and there really is a Christmas miracle because she gets up, short blonde hair sticking up all over the place, and slinks out on to the landing with an outsized jumper pulled over her mini nightie. 'Happy Christmas,' she says sleepily, and we all go downstairs together.

Mum and Paddy are already up. All traces of last night's

❀❀❀❀❀❀❀❀❀❀❀❀❀❀❀❀❀❀❀❀❀

party have been cleared away; Paddy has lit the fire, switched on the Christmas tree lights and put a CD on in the background. The knitted stockings we hung from the mantelpiece last night are lying down on the hearth, bulging with little presents, and the mince pie and the whisky Paddy said we should leave out for Santa are gone, leaving nothing but crumbs and an empty glass.

I can't help smiling.

We open our stockings, which are filled with little things like oranges and chocolate coins and glittery eyeshadow and stripy socks. Honey gives us all an instant makeover with the glittery stuff, even Cherry, and we sit in front of the fire eating chocolate coins and segments of orange and wearing our stripy socks. Then Coco begins to eye the prezzies under the tree and Mum shakes her head and says that we need to eat first, and we have half an hour to be dressed.

There's a scramble for the bathrooms but we are all ready in time, me in layered cotton petticoats with a moss-green jumper, the silver bracelets from Clara's trunk jangling, Summer in a pretty chiffony dress and pink cardi, and Cherry and Coco in variations of jeans and outsize jumpers. Honey is model-girl cute in a flower-print minidress and purple tights, her sad eyes rimmed with eyeliner.

Paddy has made pancakes for breakfast, which was one of Mum's special requests, and we eat them with sugar and lemon juice and chocolate spread, which is normally outlawed but is allowed today because it's Christmas and because Cherry asked for it specially.

Then it's present time.

Mum gets a dress and a pair of suede boots and Paddy gets new jeans and a scarf and a bunch of CDs. Cherry gets a string of cherry-blossom fairy lights for her room, and a cute mini-kimono wrap and a little blue Netbook to write her stories on. Honey gets poster paints, sketchbooks and a mobile phone to replace the one she dropped into a rock pool on the beach, back in the summer. Coco gets a book of violin tunes, a riding hat and a voucher for six riding lessons, and just about brings the roof down with excitement.

Summer gets the pointe shoes she tried on last week in town, along with a gauzy practice skirt and a fluffy pink jumper, and I get the black fringed shawl with roses embroidered on it and a huge, heavy, weirdly shaped parcel wrapped in giftwrap and tied up with ribbon.

'Careful,' Paddy says. 'You need to be gentle.'

I peel the paper away to reveal what looks like a giant shell or a horn of some kind.

'What is it?' Coco asks, screwing up her nose.

'No idea!'

My eyes widen as I pull off the rest of the wrapping to unveil an ancient gramophone with a little stack of elderly jazz records.

'Wow!' I say. 'This is amazing . . . it must be really old! I've seen pictures of things like this!'

'It's old all right,' Paddy says. 'I looked it up, and I reckon it could be from round about 1910. The records are called 78s . . . they're fragile, so be careful. There was a whole box of them, but most were broken.'

'You said you wanted a surprise,' Mum said. 'Something vintage. It's a real collector's item, I reckon!'

'I love it!'

Paddy shows me how to lift out the little handle and fit it into the side to wind up the gramophone, place a record on the turntable and lift the heavy arm across. Suddenly the disc is spinning round beneath the spiky needle and a crackly tune, surprisingly loud, spills out of the horn-shaped speaker.

'It's awesome,' I grin. 'Where did you get it?'

'You won't believe it, but it was in with all that stuff from the attic,' Mum says. 'Paddy had it in the workshop store-room, and when you mentioned wanting something special, something vintage . . . well, we thought you'd like it, so we got it fixed up!'

'I do!' I say, and I let my fingers trail across the glossy walnut casing. 1910. If this gramophone has been around since then, the chances are that Clara used it. Did her fingers stroke the wood, wind up the turntable, choose a record from the collection? I imagine her laughing, dancing in her flapper dresses, before the walls closed in around her and the dancing stopped.

Summer catches my eye, her face pale.

'It was hers, wasn't it?' she says tightly, touching the glossy walnut case. 'Clara's. I can tell. You can feel a sadness around it . . . like the dresses, the violin. Am I the only one that can sense it?'

Mum laughs. 'A sadness? I don't think so, Summer.'

❋❋❋❋❋❋❋❋❋❋❋❋❋❋❋❋❋❋❋❋❋❋❋

'Spooky,' Coco says.

Honey rolls her eyes. 'It's just a piece of junk,' she says bluntly. 'No offence. Quite pretty, maybe worth something, but trust me – there is nothing spooky about it.'

Mum puts an arm round Summer's shoulders. 'They're just things, love, beautiful things – they don't hold memories or feelings. I think that silly ghost story has upset you. It's nonsense, you know that, don't you?'

'I don't believe in ghosts,' Summer says firmly. 'I'm not crazy! But I'm telling you, there is something weird about all this stuff. It makes me uneasy.'

The record comes to an end, and I take it off and slide it back into its slipcase. 'I love it,' I tell Mum and Paddy. 'Really I do. But I won't play it when you're about, Summer, not if it upsets you.'

An awkward silence settles around us.

'There is one more present for you two,' Mum tells Summer and me. 'You mentioned that you'd like a birthday party. And thirteen is a landmark age, so we thought . . . why not? We haven't had birthday parties for years because of the B&B, but Paddy's suggested hiring the village hall so there'd be no problem of disturbing the guests . . .'

❀❀❀❀❀❀❀❀❀❀❀❀❀❀❀❀❀❀❀❀

'No way!' Summer squeals, her subdued mood evaporating instantly. 'A party! A proper, grown-up thirteenth birthday party! Seriously, that is the best present ever! Thank you!'

'Thank you,' I echo as Summer flings her arms round Mum and Paddy in turn. I dredge up a smile, but it's a shaky one. I feel like I have just unwrapped a badly knitted cardigan in bobbly orange and turquoise wool, two sizes too small, from a well-meaning great auntie. A Christmas gathering is one thing, but a birthday party – where Summer and I are centre of attention? It's the last thing I want, and I am pretty sure I said so too, when Summer first mentioned the idea. The thing is, when Summer is around my feelings and opinions seem to fade into the background.

'We can plan it all out,' Summer is saying. 'Draw up a guest list and ask everyone . . . decorate the hall. Oh, it's going to be amazing! I cannot wait! Skye, isn't this awesome?'

'Awesome,' I say, trying to inject at least a little enthusiasm into my voice. Mum and Paddy are trying to be kind, I know. And it has chased the shadows from Summer's face and put her in a great mood, which means I can stop feeling so guilty about the gramophone.

❀❀❀❀❀❀❀❀❀❀❀❀❀❀❀❀❀❀❀❀❀

Mum starts folding up wrapping paper and Paddy says he's left something out in the workshop and slips away, and when he gets back he winks at Mum which means they are definitely up to something.

'Coco?' Mum says. 'There's one present left for you . . . it's in the kitchen.'

Coco's eyes open wide. 'What is it? Is it a pony?'

Paddy laughs. 'In the kitchen?'

'You never know,' she says. 'My friend Amy says that you and Mum are quite eccentric, so anything is possible, right?'

She runs to the kitchen with us at her heels, and right at the door a thin whickering sound peals out, and we begin to wonder if the pony idea is actually as far-fetched as it sounds.

And then we're inside, and there is no pony, but a big cardboard box has appeared in front of the Aga and we crowd round and the sound peals out again and this time it is very definitely a bleat.

'A lamb!' Coco squeals. 'A baby LAMB!'

'An orphan,' Paddy says. 'She was born down at Joe's, yesterday. He has some New Year's lambs every year, but this one was extra early and her mum didn't make it. Joe says he doesn't have a foster-mum for her, or the time or the space to raise her by hand. So we thought that maybe you might –'

'YESSS!' Coco yelps, leaning down to wrap her arms round the tiny lamb. 'Oh, thank you! Thank you!'

22

It's chaos after that, with Coco learning how to make up little bottles of milk to feed the lamb and Mum cooking and Paddy chopping vegetables for lunch and Fred the dog sticking his head over the top of the cardboard box every few minutes to suss out the newcomer.

Paddy tries to explain that the lamb can't actually live in a box in the kitchen once the B&B is open again, and that he's cleared out one of the old stables next to the workshop, but Coco isn't listening. She manages to wrap the lamb in a blanket and brings it into the living room where we're loafing about eating chocolate coins and trying to think up names for her while watching *A Christmas Carol* on TV.

✿✿✿✿✿✿✿✿✿✿✿✿✿✿✿✿✿✿✿✿✿✿

'What about Holly?' I say. 'It should be something Christmassy!'

'Woolly Jumper,' Summer suggests. 'Because she is.'

'How about Mint Sauce?' Cherry teases, and Coco throws a cushion at her.

The lamb lets out a long, plaintive baaa and that's when the onscreen Scrooge says 'Bah, humbug,' and we all agree that the only possible name for a lamb born at Christmas is Humbug.

We're having so much fun it's like we're a proper family. I can almost forget the weirdness of the past few months. Almost.

Then Honey yells at us from the breakfast room. 'Hey! I've got Dad on Skype! Quick, come and talk to him!'

Summer, Coco and I run through – Coco with Humbug still in her arms. Honey has Mum's laptop on one of the breakfast tables, and filling the screen is an image of Dad, tanned and smiling in a blue shirt. My heart hurts, suddenly, unexpectedly.

'He wanted to talk to you,' Honey says, as if she might have hogged him all to herself otherwise.

'Dad!' Summer says. 'How are you? Is it hot there?'

'Happy Christmas!' Coco says. 'I've got a lamb!'

Honey nudges me, but all I can do is smile and bite my lip and hope that I won't cry.

'My girls!' Dad grins. 'Let me have a look at you!'

He leans forward and the picture dissolves, then reappears again. 'Summer! Skye! You're looking so grown up! What are you, almost twelve now?'

'Almost thirteen,' I whisper, and the words seem to stick in my throat because my own dad doesn't know how old we are.

'Amazing,' Dad says. 'And Coco . . . still animal mad, I see! Where did you get that lamb from?'

'It was a present!' Coco says, and Dad shakes his head and says Mum must be crazy.

'What time is it in Australia?' Summer asks.

'It's evening now . . . Christmas is almost over, here. We had Christmas lunch down on the beach! You'd love it here, girls! Always sunny, and a real land of opportunity. You'll have to come out and visit!'

'We will!' Honey says, all smiles. 'Did you get your presents?'

'Yeah, yeah . . . great, thanks, girls!' he says, as if he can't

❀❀❀❀❀❀❀❀❀❀❀❀❀❀❀❀❀❀❀❀

even remember the gifts we each spent so long making, choosing, buying. Dad's parcel was wrapped and ready on the first of December, ready to go long before the last posting date to Australia because we didn't want any chance of it being late.

'I didn't have time to get you anything,' Dad adds apologetically. 'Still settling in . . . I'll send some money!'

'Could we come out to visit soon?' Honey presses. 'I'd love to see Australia, it has to be better than this dump. When would be a good time?'

He laughs. 'Better wait until we've settled in a bit,' he says. 'Give your mum a chance to save up the air fares!'

Honey's face falls. We all know that Dad has plenty of cash to spare, but Mum has hardly any, and what she does have is spent on us or ploughed back into the business. If we have to save our own air fares, it's going to take a very long time indeed.

Dad yawns. 'Girls, it's been great talking to you, but I have to go . . . things to do . . . Merry Christmas!'

'Do you want to speak to Mum?' Honey says. 'I'll go and tell her –'

'No, don't bother,' he says quickly. 'I'll give her a ring in a day or two . . .'

❀❀❀❀❀❀❀❀❀❀❀❀❀❀❀❀❀❀❀❀❀

There's the sound of someone talking in the background and Dad smiles and waves and the screen goes dead as he cuts the connection. We stare at the silent laptop, slightly stunned.

'Things to do?' Summer says. 'What things?'

I put an arm round her shoulder and she wipes a hand across her eyes, then smiles bravely. It's the first time in months where I look at her and think maybe we are not so different after all.

'There was someone there with him,' Coco frowns. 'And did you notice, he kept saying "we". Like, *we had Christmas lunch down on the beach*. And *wait until we've settled in a bit*. Do you think he's got a girlfriend?'

'No way,' Honey says. 'He wouldn't.'

I'm pretty sure he would.

After Christmas dinner, minus the sprouts and with added nut roast in honour of Coco, the awkward, sad feeling of talking to Dad begins to fade. We decide to use Skype again, this time to talk to Grandma Kate and her husband Jules over in France.

Mum sets the laptop on the coffee table, and we crowd

round, still in our paper hats from the crackers we've pulled, perched on the squashy blue sofa, Humbug included. Last year Grandma Kate and Jules came over for Christmas, but this year they won't be over until the wedding so we won't see them properly for ages.

Grandma Kate has sent over a little parcel of presents with *Do not open until instructed* written on the back. She says she wanted to see our faces and we can open them now. Grandma Kate and Jules munch on the chocolates we sent them, modelling the hats and scarves that made up the rest of their prezzie.

It is kind of chaotic, with everyone talking at once and wishing each other a Happy Christmas and Humbug bleating loudly. We open our prezzies, which turn out to be silver charm bracelets – Honey's has an artist's palette charm, Coco's a little horseshoe, Cherry's has cherries, Summer's a pair of ballet shoes and mine a little silver bird.

My heart flips over.

'I'm sorry yours isn't very inspired, Skye,' Grandma Kate says. 'I was looking for something with a vintage feel, but then I saw the bird, and somehow I thought of you. There's no particular reason, but . . . well, it just felt right!'

❀❀❀❀❀❀❀❀❀❀❀❀❀❀❀❀❀❀❀❀❀

The little bird is exactly right, more right than anything else she could have chosen.

'I love it!' I tell her. 'It's perfect!'

It is, because it reminds me of Finch.

23

It's almost sunset and Finch and I are climbing the hill behind the village, the tawny lurcher racing on ahead, our shadows trailing behind across the daisy-strewn grass. The day is warm and the walk is steep, and somewhere along the way Finch takes hold of my hand, pulling me along, and we finally make it right to the top.

The breeze lifts our hair and ruffles our clothes and we look right out over the village, over the bay, at the silver-blue ocean that stretches on forever. We sit for a while and talk, still holding hands, watching as the light turns to pink and yellow and gold, as the sun drops gently into the sea.

In my dreams, there are no unwanted thirteenth birthday parties to plan, no boy-crazy best friends, no stroppy, off-the-rails older sister, no boy mates who just happen to be in love with my too-perfect twin. No wonder I'm hooked on being there. My dream world is a whole lot less stressy than the real one.

On New Year's Eve, while the rest of the family are curled up on the squashy blue sofas watching back-to-back Harry Potter DVDs, I am in my room, hunting for the lost letters – again. For the hundredth time I check the desk, the trunk, the dressing-table drawers. I search under the beds, in the wardrobe, on the bookshelf, but find nothing. It's as if they never existed.

Summer puts her head round the door. 'Skye?' she says. 'You OK?'

'I'm searching for Clara's letters,' I sigh. I have asked Summer about them a couple of times since the day they went missing, but she has always said she hasn't a clue where they might be. She's so weird about everything to do with Clara I don't want to push it, but I have to ask one last time. 'Summer, are you absolutely sure you haven't seen them?'

'I don't know.' She shrugs. 'I don't remember, OK? Could Mum have chucked them out?'

I eye the wastepaper basket. 'I don't think so. She wouldn't. Would she?'

'Might have,' Summer shrugs. 'She's so busy lately, she might not have been paying attention. Anyway, forget those stupid letters, Skye, please! I swear, it's like you're obsessed! Come downstairs – we're just about to start *Harry Potter and the Prisoner of Azkaban*. Mum's made popcorn . . .'

I go with her to keep the peace, and in the end we stay up till midnight, our eyes square from too many DVDs, our bellies full of pizza and popcorn. Seconds before the clock strikes twelve we run outside to wish each other a Happy New Year, singing 'Auld Lang Syne' to the sound of Coco on the violin, which is pretty painful but fun all the same. All of us except for Honey, anyway, who has gone to a New Year's party down in the village and isn't back yet.

There are fireworks going off in the distance somewhere, and the stars hang above us in a velvet sky as we hug and laugh and pretend that Coco's playing isn't hurting our ears.

'I'm going to practise even more from now on,' Coco says as we head upstairs to bed. 'It's my New Year's Resolution.'

'Right,' Cherry says politely.

'Great,' Summer adds through gritted teeth.

'I might be a famous violinist,' Coco muses. 'One day.'

'Go to bed, titch,' I sigh. 'Happy New Year, you lot.'

❀❀❀❀❀❀❀❀❀❀❀❀❀❀❀❀❀❀❀❀❀

'Happy New Year,' they echo as we part on the landing. 'Goodnight!'

Summer and I are almost ready for bed when the racket starts up. It sounds like cats being strangled, or fingernails scraping down an old-fashioned blackboard, or the wails of a hundred screeching banshees.

'Oh no!' I exclaim. 'She's playing that wretched violin!'

'Sheesh,' Summer growls. 'I wish Paddy had never found all that stuff in the attic. Some things are better left alone. There's you with those creepy dresses, and Coco with a violin that sounds like someone being murdered . . .'

Summer puts a pillow over her head. 'It's painful,' she says, in a slightly muffled voice. 'Make it go away!'

But Coco's violin playing does not go away.

'Leave her,' I sigh. 'Cherry probably can't hear it like we can, and Honey's out . . . when does she ever have a chance to practise, with the B&B guests around? Give her five minutes!'

Summer drops the pillow and slaps her hands over her ears, and my heart slows.

Where the pillows have shifted, I glimpse the corner of a faded blue bundle.

176

'Summer!' I say, my voice unsteady. 'What's that under your pillow?'

'What?' Summer says, but she blinks at me like a startled rabbit caught in the headlights.

I go over to her bed and yank out a slim stack of envelopes tied up with ribbon, addressed to Clara Travers in a bold, sloping script.

'The missing letters!' I say. 'You told me you hadn't seen them, but you had them all the time! You lied to me!'

'Not on purpose!' Summer protests, but her cheeks are pink with guilt. 'I was just curious. You've been so obsessed with stupid Clara Travers. It's all you care about these days. It's weird, Skye, can't you see? I just read a couple of the letters, but they were so dull . . .'

'But you said you didn't remember seeing them, that they'd probably been thrown away.'

'I wish they had been,' Summer says.

'I don't get it. Why would you lie?'

Her eyes flash with anger. 'I was worried, OK?' she snaps. 'You've changed, since you got those stupid clothes. You know I think they're creepy, but you don't seem to care, and now you've got that ugly old gramophone it's even worse!

❀❀❀❀❀❀❀❀❀❀❀❀❀❀❀❀❀❀❀❀❀❀❀

It's spooky, Skye. Remember that dream you told me about, where you dreamt of Clara and the gypsies and woke up all upset and confused? I took them because I was worried! Your eyes are all faraway and dreamy half the time, like you've got a secret. It scares me. We never used to have secrets!'

'You never used to lie to me either,' I say coldly.

'For God's sake!' Summer yells, turning away from me. 'That horrible noise is hurting my head!' She picks up an old knitted rabbit, a toy we've shared since we were toddlers, and chucks it at the door. Coco's violin practice creaks on anyhow.

'I mean it, you know,' Summer says. 'It's as if you're hiding something from me. I can tell!'

I can't meet her eyes. I guess I am hiding a lot from Summer – more than I ever would have done before. The fact I am falling for Finch, a boy who may or may not be a ghost; Alfie, with his secret crush; my worries about Millie; and the way I am feeling overshadowed by my twin.

I just don't know what to do about it. I don't want to share Finch because he is something that is mine alone, something special, and I couldn't bear it if Summer freaked

❀❀❀❀❀❀❀❀❀❀❀❀❀❀❀❀❀❀❀

out at the idea of me crushing on a ghost boy. As for Alfie, I promised to keep his secret – I can't go back on that. And how do I explain how I'm feeling about Millie when Summer is actually part of the problem?

Tears sting my eyes, but I won't, can't let them fall.

'Taking the letters . . . it was stupid, I know,' she admits. 'It's just . . . you're more interested in this stupid Clara Travers than in me, lately. I feel like I'm losing you, sometimes. You're always with Cherry or that annoying Alfie Anderson, or else you're mooning about over the gramophone or the dresses, thinking about some girl who's been dead for almost a century. I hate it! You used to listen to me, you used to need me . . .'

Sudden anger flares up inside me. For as long as I can remember, it has always been about what Summer wants, what Summer needs. She cannot possibly be jealous that I am spending time with Cherry, my own stepsister, or Alfie, because she doesn't even like him. Summer has no shortage of friends herself. She has even collected Millie up . . . my best friend.

To start with, a part of me really did believe that Alfie Anderson might like me, and even though I'd rather have

179

a dream boy than a clown, it still hurt to know that even he prefers my sister to me. I am just good old Skye, who wears funny clothes, who is a loyal friend and a good listener and once mummified her Barbie doll with toilet roll. Which twin would you choose, if you were Alfie?

Resentment curls inside me, a feeling I am not proud of. If I'm honest, it's not just resentment but envy too. Summer is the talented one, the one who shines.

Across the landing, the violin screeches out a jarring, unearthly soundtrack to our argument. The last person to play that violin may well have been Clara Travers, and I shiver at the thought.

'I just have a bad feeling about all this,' Summer says. 'The spooky story, the letters, the clothes. And I had a dream too, like the ones you had. A really weird dream . . .'

The anger melts away and my heart stills. 'You did?' I whisper. 'What kind of dream?'

If twins can think the same thoughts, feel the same feelings, then maybe they can dream the same dreams too?

But Summer's eyes brim with tears.

'It wasn't a dream exactly,' she says. 'More of a nightmare. I know it wasn't real, but it felt that way . . . I can't explain . . .'

'A nightmare?'

She bites her lip. 'It was horrible,' she tells me. 'I was dreaming about Clara Travers, and she was wearing the green dress and the coat from the trunk. She was running through the woods, looking for someone . . . crying . . . and when she turned to look at me, I realized it wasn't Clara Travers at all. It was you. And then everything changed and you were underwater, struggling, drowning, and I was calling your name but you couldn't hear. It was horrible, Skye, you have to believe me . . .'

My scalp prickles and a shiver runs down my spine. A dream like that would be enough to frighten anyone.

'I do believe you,' I whisper. 'But it's not real, Summer. Just a nightmare.'

'It felt real!' she argues. 'It felt like a warning! I know it's crazy, but what if there really is a ghost, and she's angry at you for wearing her dresses? What if she actually died in that green dress, and now she's trying to make you do the same things she did?'

I've wondered whether the dreams could be some kind

of echo from the past, evidence that Clara was reaching out to me, pulling me into her story, but the idea of that has never scared me before. Now I can't help wondering if Summer is right, if I am losing myself in it all.

Could Clara actually be angry that I am wearing her velvet flapper dresses, falling for her gypsy boy? Will my dreams end in nightmares of drowning, death? No wonder my twin hates the old clothes, the gramophone.

'Hey,' I say, moving across to sit beside her. 'Clara didn't die in the green dress, or the coat . . . they wouldn't be here if she had, would they? Her body was never found.'

'I suppose . . .'

'And we don't believe in ghosts, remember? We've just scared ourselves, that's all. Mum and Paddy found the trunk on Halloween, just after we'd been telling that ghost story. Face it, Summer, you and I both have very strong imagination. That's not always a good thing!'

Summer nods, taking a deep breath in.

'Skye . . . you're not still having dreams about Clara, are you?' she asks.

I am, of course. Every night now, the dreams come, marshmallow sweet and softer than reality, dreams where

I can't figure out if I am Skye Tanberry or Clara Travers. Does Summer need to know that?

'No,' I lie to my twin. 'No more dreams.'

Out on the landing we hear a creak of footsteps. Honey, home from her party, bangs on Coco's bedroom door and yells at her to stop the racket, and at last the violin's wails fade and die.

I wipe Summer's tears away. 'C'mon. It's a whole new year,' I whisper. 'Let's not fight.'

'No,' Summer sighs. 'That's the last thing I want.'

I bite my lip and hope the New Year will wipe out the tensions and resentments. A fresh start – that's exactly what me and my sister need.

24

Much later, once Summer is asleep, I switch on my bedside lamp and read through the letters. There have to be some answers to the mystery here. Who is Finch? Did Clara fall in love with him? What happened between them, at the end? And why do I seem to be reliving it all in my dreams?

I think briefly about what Summer said, about me being obsessed. She's right, I know. My dream world is soft and sweet and comforting, like the taste of marshmallows . . . but it's sticky too, and just as addictive. I can't seem to find my way out of it, and even I find that slightly worrying. I'm pretty sure that the only way I can stop the dreams is to find some answers . . .

But the letters are not from Finch, of course. A Romany

traveller boy who'd probably never even been to school . . . he wouldn't be big on writing, I guess. No, the letters are from Harry, the stern-faced man in the locket photograph. They are love letters, old-fashioned and formal and achingly dull.

Slowly I piece together a picture. Harry and Clara met in London, at the house of family friends. He drove down to see her, taking her out for a drive in his Austin Twenty motor car, and after that there were dinners and house parties and theatre trips and presents. A locket, a powder compact with butterflies on the lid, a tame linnet in a cage.

I blink. Could it be? Across the room, the vintage powder-blue birdcage hangs in the darkness, a few curling tendrils from the climbing plant inside it silhouetted in the moonlight. The birdcage . . . that was Clara's too. Summer can't have bothered to read that far. How would she feel if she knew?

I read on.

The last present of all is an engagement ring, and soon after that, wedding plans and talk of how Clara would come to live in London, and how there wouldn't be quite so many theatre trips and parties then because of course there would be budgets to keep and a household to run and children to consider.

I shiver. Did Clara ever look at the tame linnet in its pretty powder-blue cage and feel every bit as trapped? I am not sure what a linnet is, exactly, but from the letters I gather it is a wild bird, a songbird, small and bright and beautiful. I don't think many people would want to keep a wild bird captive, these days, but perhaps things were different back then. Perhaps it was just the way things were, like girls getting married at seventeen because it was expected of them?

I don't know Clara's reasons for saying yes to her fiancé, but as I read I can feel the prison walls closing in around her. Did she feel it too? Was that why she fell for a gypsy boy and the promise of a life on the road?

I fold the letters, tie them up again with ribbon, switch off the lamp. I think maybe my sister is right, and I am getting a little too hung up on a sad story from the past, tangled up in shadows from long ago. Summer's nightmare worries me – not because I think it means anything sinister, but because it shows how skewed things are becoming.

I am spending way too much time thinking about Clara,

❀❀❀❀❀❀❀❀❀❀❀❀❀❀❀❀❀❀❀❀❀❀

wearing her clothes, imagining her life, her story, the boy she loved, the man she didn't. Dreaming her dreams.

I wanted to find the letters so much because I thought they would help . . . but they've just deepened the mystery. I need to find out who Finch is and why he is haunting my dreams because, until I know, I am not going to be able to let go of him.

25

January feels like the longest month since time began. The weather is grey and cold and endlessly wet and even the teachers are depressed and grumpy, except for Mr Wolfe, who pins a lifesize *Dr Who* poster up on the classroom door and starts dressing the part too, wearing a bow tie to class. It's not a good look.

Interestingly, though, he has graduated from everyone's favourite teacher to torment to everyone's favourite teacher, full stop. 'He's a dude,' Alfie shrugs, which may be partly because the two of them bonded over the whole flying rucksack incident, or maybe because Alfie is a big fan of *Dr Who*.

He cannot resist the occasional tease, of course. Old habits die hard. 'What's the time, Mr Wolfe?' is Alfie's favourite greeting to our history teacher these days, reminding me of the playground game we had at Kitnor Primary. I think he is waiting for Mr Wolfe to say, 'Dinner time!'

A couple of weeks into the new term, Mr Wolfe brandishes his new sonic screwdriver at the class and announces we are having a surprise history quiz. There are groans of dismay because nobody has revised, but Mr Wolfe says that the questions are random, some based on things we've been studying and some not.

There is a prize, a huge bar of chocolate, and Mr Wolfe says we can use any method we like to find the answers providing we stay inside the classroom.

'This quiz is to show you that history can be fun,' Mr Wolfe says. 'I want you to be time travellers. We may not have time machines or sonic screwdrivers in real life, but we can find other ways to unlock the secrets of the past. Books, letters, photos, paintings, objects . . . all of those things can help. Be time detectives – use any evidence you can find to piece together the answers.'

I blink. That's what I need to be – a time detective, solving the mystery of Clara and Finch. It's like Mr Wolfe says,

✿✿✿✿✿✿✿✿✿✿✿✿✿✿✿✿✿✿✿✿✿✿✿

it's just a case of finding the evidence and piecing it together. And now I know the letters can't help me, I need to find some more clues.

There is a scramble for the three classroom computers, and the place goes into meltdown as pupils ransack the stock cupboard, leafing wildly through books and sorting through the topic boxes. 'Can we use mobiles, Sir?' Alfie asks, and Mr Wolfe says yes, but not to wave them about too much in case Mr King comes in, as we are not actually supposed to have them switched on in school.

'Cool,' Alfie says, taking out an iPhone to google for the answers while other kids try ringing home for help.

I scan through the quiz, my mind elsewhere.

Which British leader abolished Christmas?

Who was Hereward the Wake?

What is a palaeontologist?

Mr Wolfe is a teacher who believes in time travel, who thinks that all of us can be history detectives. If anyone could help me sort facts from fiction on the Clara story, it would be him. I abandon my quiz and wander over to his desk.

'Everything OK, Skye?' he asks, smiling at me over half-moon spectacles. 'Not finished already, surely?'

❀❀❀❀❀❀❀❀❀❀❀❀❀❀❀❀❀❀❀

'Um . . . yes, Sir,' I say.

All around me, my classmates are showing a real feeling for history too. Millie is wearing a papier-mâché Viking helmet rescued from the stock cupboard and Summer is twirling about the room in a red cloak and a crown taken from the 'Kings & Queens' topic box. Kids are sitting on tabletops, talking on mobiles, leafing through textbooks, gathered round the computers, some of them wearing chain mail or top hats.

'It was Cromwell, trust me,' someone is saying. 'My dad mentioned it over the holidays . . .'

'What's a wake, anyway?'

'Hang on, hang on, I'm googling it . . .'

'It's the study of birds, isn't it?'

'No, no, that's ornithology. That's got nothing to do with history . . .'

If Mr King were to stick his head round the door, it would look like chaos, but I think it is a good kind of chaos.

Mr Wolfe raises an eyebrow. 'So, Skye? Can I help?'

I swallow. 'I haven't finished the quiz yet, Sir, but . . . I wanted to ask you something . . .'

'Ask away,' he says.

I look around, but nobody is listening. 'Do you believe in ghosts, Sir?'

Mr Wolfe raises an eyebrow. 'That's a loaded question,' he says. 'I haven't actually seen any myself, Skye. But then again, I wouldn't rule anything out. History can leave a long shadow on the present day, I know that much. Who knows? Why? Have you seen something?'

A blush creeps into my cheeks. I haven't, of course, not really. A dream is very different from a ghostly figure in white who glides through walls and makes the temperature plummet down below zero. And wasn't I the one telling Summer a few weeks ago that ghosts don't exist?

'No, no, of course not,' I say, backtracking. 'It's just that there's a ghost story in our family I would like to investigate. I'd like to find out more of the details, but I don't know where to look . . . or who to ask. I mean, there might not be any information out there . . .'

'What kind of dates are we talking?' Mr Wolfe wants to know. 'If it's nineteenth- or twentieth-century stuff, Kitnor Museum may be able to help. They hold quite a lot of information there. Parish records of births, deaths, marriages . . . old newspapers . . . even some old diaries

❀❀❀❀❀❀❀❀❀❀❀❀❀❀❀❀❀❀❀❀

and household account books. I can't promise miracles, but you should find something about your ghost story.'

'Thanks, Sir,' I grin. 'I'll try that.'

'YESSSS!' Alfie Anderson whoops from the back of the class, his new cool-boy persona forgotten in the heat of the moment. 'I've done it, Sir – finished! That chocolate bar is MINE!'

That, of course, is a miracle in itself.

I haven't been to Kitnor Museum since I was nine or ten. It's small and quiet and dusty, with strange shop dummies from the 1960s dressed in home-made costumes to look like smugglers and highwaymen and Victorian ladies. There are displays of old photographs and paintings, a couple of bits of ancient furniture and assorted china, handmade lace and broken clay pipes locked up in glass cases.

I manage to sneak off after school without anyone asking too many questions. Summer has a ballet class and Millie hasn't wanted to come over to Tanglewood or hang out in the village for weeks now, which at least means I don't have to give her any excuses.

Still, by the time I get to the museum it's almost closing

time, and the place is deserted except for a smiley woman with dark frizzy hair sorting through some old papers at the desk. As she works, she reaches out and selects a chocolate from the box beside her, and I almost laugh out loud because they are Chocolate Box truffles, our chocolates.

'Excuse me,' I ask. 'I wonder if you can help me? I'm trying to find out about a girl who lived in Kitnor in the 1920s . . .'

She looks up. 'Oh, you're one of the Chocolate Box Girls!' she says, delighted. 'One of the Tanberrys, yes? I saw you and your sisters in the magazine, and I've spotted you in the village once or twice.'

She picks up the box of truffles. 'My boyfriend gave me these for Christmas,' she says. 'They're the best chocolates I've ever tasted!'

'I'll tell Mum,' I say.

'Yes, do. So . . . you're trying to trace someone from the 1920s? We're about to close, but I was planning on working late anyway. Let's take a look at the parish records.'

Searching through the records, I tell the museum lady the story of Clara Travers and about the trunk Mum and Paddy found. 'You have her dresses?' she asks. 'Really? And

194

hats and shoes and bracelets and letters? They'd make an amazing exhibit, if you wanted to lend them to the museum at any point!'

'Maybe,' I frown. 'If I could just find out what actually happened . . .'

The idea of parting with the dresses feels uncomfortable, and I can see for a tiny moment why Summer doesn't like my attachment to them. They're not my dresses, after all – why shouldn't I share them? I'm worried if I do it'll mean giving up the dreams, that's why.

Half an hour later, we've found an entry for the birth of Clara Jane Travers from the year 1909, daughter of William Henry Travers and Elizabeth Mary Travers of Tanglewood House.

'If your story's right, and she was seventeen when she died, that would make it 1926,' the museum lady says. 'But there's no record here of her death, or of her marriage either, obviously. I'm guessing that the death wasn't recorded, perhaps because her body was never found. Let's see if the newspaper archives have anything . . .'

But when we look through the newspaper reports, there are no mentions of a death by drowning, no references to

❀❀❀❀❀❀❀❀❀❀❀❀❀❀❀❀❀❀❀❀❀❀❀

suicide. 'I'm sorry I can't be of more help,' the museum lady says. 'Perhaps it was covered up to spare the family the scandal? They'd have tried to keep something like that out of the newspapers.'

'Well, we tried,' I say. 'I have a photograph of Clara's fiancé, but he didn't live in Kitnor so there's no point in looking for him. I don't suppose there's any way to trace the gypsies?'

'Doubtful,' the museum lady sighs. 'They lived outside society, for the most part. They rarely recorded births, deaths or marriages because they moved around so much.

'We do know that the Romanies used the woods by Tanglewood House as a stopping-off point until the 1920s. After that, they switched to the pastures down by Kitnor Quay. Perhaps that was because the Travers family warned them off, as your story says? It's a pity we don't have a name to work on . . .'

'Finch,' I say, although I have no proof that the boy from my dreams has anything to do with Clara Travers. My cheeks glow pink. 'I mean . . . it could be Finch, possibly, but I have no evidence. Just . . . something I'd heard.'

'Do you have a first name?' she asks.

❀❀❀❀❀❀❀❀❀❀❀❀❀❀❀❀❀❀❀❀❀❀

I frown. 'No . . . no first name. Sorry.'

'Well, leave it with me. I'll take a look at the local farm records from the 1920s and let you know if I find anything.'

Abruptly, the door flies open and a tall, dishevelled figure wearing a tweed jacket and yellow corduroy trousers bowls in, wrestling a dripping umbrella.

'Grace!' he says, flinging his arms round the museum lady.

'Charlie!'

Mr Wolfe catches my eye over his girlfriend's shoulder, and his face reddens.

'Ah . . . Skye, how nice to see you . . . you took my advice then!'

'Yes, Sir,' I grin. 'Guess I'd better be going. Um . . . what's the time, Mr Wolfe?'

'Almost six, I think . . .'

'Dinner time,' I say, grinning, and sprint for the door.

Alfie Anderson would be proud of me.

26

'Sorted,' Mum says, putting down the phone. 'It's all booked. The village hall, Thursday 14 February, eight till late . . . the best birthday party of the season!'

It's the following day after school, and Summer, Cherry and I are all in the kitchen, finishing up homework before dinner.

'Brilliant!' Summer whoops. 'Can we invite everyone? All the kids in our year? And all the girls from the dance school, as well?'

'I don't see why not!'

'And some of the boys from the high school?' Summer checks. 'Not that I am interested in boys, obviously, but some of the other girls might like that . . .'

❀❀❀❀❀❀❀❀❀❀❀❀❀❀❀❀❀❀❀❀❀

'Shay could do the sound for you,' Cherry volunteers. 'He's really good.'

'Definitely,' Summer says. 'We can make playlists, and have a Valentine's theme with pink streamers and pink lemonade, and a big pink cake shaped like a heart . . .'

'Skye?' Mum says, ruffling my hair. 'Does that sound OK? It's your party too, after all!'

I bite my lip.

The last time Summer and I had a birthday party we were nine years old and still into egg sandwiches and mini pizzas and those hedgehog things made out of cheese and pineapple on cocktail sticks. That was the year Alfie ate all the sausage rolls and most of the trifle and had to be sick in the bathroom; the year we had a Barbie Princess cake where the Barbie doll was sticking up out of the iced sponge, all piped with butter-cream ruffles to look like a crinoline gown.

I remember my blue party dress and Summer's pink one, and the way Mum used to cheat when she stopped the music for Pass the Parcel, so that everyone got one of the tiny presents she'd wrapped up between each layer of tissue paper.

I used to love those parties, but a thirteenth birthday party is not the same kind of thing at all. I think things have moved on a bit since then, into territory I am not so sure of.

'Brilliant,' I say, as brightly as I can. 'I mean . . . cool. Does it have to be a Valentine's theme, though? Not everyone's going to like all that romance stuff . . .'

Like me, for example.

'Of course they will,' Summer says flatly. 'It's on Valentine's Day, so it's the obvious theme, right?'

'We could do a vintage thing instead,' I suggest. 'People could wear really cool vintage fashions, and –'

'Skye!' my twin says, rolling her eyes. 'You are history obsessed! Trust me, people will not want to dress up in jumble-sale relics for a party. It's just another excuse for you to wear one of those creepy old dresses, isn't it?'

'I love vintage!' I argue. 'What's wrong with that? It's got nothing to do with Clara's dresses.'

That's not strictly true, of course. I love Clara's dresses and wearing them makes me think of the dreams, of Finch. As if I need reminding.

'How about we make the theme Vintage Valentine?'

❀❀❀❀❀❀❀❀❀❀❀❀❀❀❀❀❀❀❀❀❀❀

Mum says brightly. 'That would be really different! Compromise, girls. It's a shared party, so both of you should have some input.'

Summer looks slightly sulky, but raises one eyebrow as if considering the idea. 'OK . . .' she says finally. 'I suppose.'

'I could do us some retro invites,' I offer. 'I suppose the vintage dress code could be optional . . .'

'No, no, we'll go for it,' Summer says, suddenly warming to the idea. 'You could help me turn that flower hairclip into a 1920s headband, Skye. I could look for a vintage-style dress . . . but not an actual ancient one, if you know what I mean!'

'I can sense a shopping trip coming on,' Mum groans. 'What have I started? Good job the January sales are still on!'

'Sounds as if it'll liven up February a bit, anyway,' Cherry says. 'And Valentine's Day is in the half-term break, so we'll have tons of time to get everything ready. I can't wait!'

Summer swipes my cloche hat from the coat rack, pulls it on and does a comedy-Charleston dance around the kitchen, making everyone laugh.

❀❀❀❀❀❀❀❀❀❀❀❀❀❀❀❀❀❀❀❀❀

'Trust me,' she says. 'This is going to be the best party this village has ever seen.'

For the party invites, I make a collage design of old records with musical notes and little hearts and a cool 1920s couple dancing. On the back we add in the venue, the date, the time and the dress code, and print out a whole bunch of them on Mum's printer.

Cherry and Coco take some to give to their friends, Shay gets a bundle to hand to his mates and even Honey says she'll invite a few people.

Our friends at school love the idea, especially when they suss that Shay is doing the music and that boys from the high school will be there.

'I seriously cannot wait,' Millie tells me. 'A proper teenage party, in a hall, with hot boys . . .'

'Hot boys might be stretching it a bit far,' I say, watching Alfie Anderson and Sid Sharma waltz across the lunch hall with their party invites between their teeth.

'They're both pretty good-looking,' Millie considers. 'It's not just your birthday, Skye, it is Valentine's Day too, and we cannot afford to be too choosy.'

'I think we can,' I say. 'Sid and Alfie are definitely not what I am looking for.'

'What *are* you looking for then?' Millie wants to know. 'Because I have to tell you, a knight in shining armour is not going to turn up at your thirteenth birthday party. You have to be more realistic.'

'Why?' I ask. 'I am a romantic. I don't want to settle for second best. And anyway, I do not want a knight in shining armour. There aren't any left, these days, are there?'

'Exactly,' Millie says. 'I know you are into all that history stuff, Skye, but don't let life pass you by. Boys don't go for history geeks.'

I grit my teeth. Millie barely bothers to conceal her irritation with me these days. We are drifting apart and we don't know what to do about it. Millie's magazines suggest talking things through. I'm not sure I'm ready for that, but I told Cherry I'd make an effort and I know I will have to try.

'Why don't you come over one day at half-term?' I ask Millie brightly. 'We can . . . um . . . try out make-up ideas or something. For the party. And talk, and just hang out, like we used to.'

'Maybe,' Millie shrugs, unimpressed. 'Will Summer be there?'

'I don't know!' I huff. 'Does it matter?'

'Suppose not. I was thinking . . . I might send Alfie a Valentine's card,' Millie muses. 'Or Sid. Just in case I don't manage to hook up with one of the high school boys, obviously.'

'Obviously.'

'Oh, there's Summer!' Millie squeaks, her face lighting up. 'I just want to ask her what I should wear. Honestly, this party is going to be SO cool, Skye. Everyone's talking about it . . .'

She runs off across the dinner hall, leaving me alone with my bowl of cold sponge pudding and custard. I am clearly too clueless to advise on fashion, even fashion with a vintage theme, and too dull to stick with for a whole lunchbreak.

I used to be the kind of girl who got on with everybody. I saw the best in people, knew how to make them smile, how to smooth down any dispute, keep everyone happy. Lately, I seem to have lost the knack . . . with Millie and my sisters, at any rate.

Millie is right about one thing, though. Everybody is

❀❀❀❀❀❀❀❀❀❀❀❀❀❀❀❀❀❀❀❀❀

talking about the party. It's like a little flash of fun in the middle of a long, grey winter.

And we're definitely in need of some fun. We're in the middle of another boom in the chocolate ordering, which means no let up in the hours spent packaging up boxes after school, thanks to a pre-Valentine's ad that Paddy put in the magazine. And then Mum and Paddy get a letter from the high school to say that Honey's grades are slipping, that her attitude in class is appalling. They go into school to talk to the teachers, and when they come back a huge row blows up.

'You have GCSEs to study for next year,' Mum says angrily. 'And unless you get your act together you are going to fail them, Honey. I thought you wanted to go to art college? Don't throw it all away!'

Honey scowls and shrugs.

'You can do better than this,' Paddy says. 'Get some help with maths and science. Start working. Ditch the late nights and the boyfriends.'

'You can't tell me –' Honey begins, but Mum interrupts.

'He can, actually,' she says. 'And he's right, Honey, we've had enough. Unless your next school report is a good one,

I will find you a different school, an all-girls' one, a board-ing school maybe. I don't know – but I will not let you mess your life up, Honey. I mean it.'

'You can't!' she screeches. 'That's blackmail! Boarding school? That's barbaric!'

'We can,' Mum says simply. 'And we will, if we have to. Shape up, Honey, show us you can do it. Good grades, or things are going to change around here. You've pushed me too far this time.'

For once, Honey doesn't have a thing to say.

27

After a couple of weeks of dull, damp January weather, the temperature drops again. The heating goes on the blink at school, and in some classrooms we take to keeping our hats and coats on. The playground is like an ice rink. To add insult to injury, a flu bug is doing the rounds. Every classroom is filled with sneezing, coughing kids, or else not filled at all because so many people are off sick.

'I hope this flu thing goes away,' Millie says. 'Or else your party is going to be in trouble. You don't want to be serving up hot lemon drinks and boxes of tissues.'

'There's more than a week to go,' I say. 'People will be better by then. They'll have half-term to recover.'

'I hope so,' Millie says. 'Because I am definitely not kissing Aaron Jones if he's snuffling and coughing like that. When you think about it, kissing is very unhygienic. All those germs. Yuck!'

'How do you know Aaron will want to kiss you, anyway?' I ask.

'I am practising my flirting techniques,' Millie says. 'I am wearing the dress I got for Christmas, because it's gorgeous, and Mum says it does look a bit vintage, in a boho-chic kind of way, and Summer thinks I should team it with strappy sandals. So I am going for a sixties hippy-chick look, and Aaron will not be able to resist me. Or Sid. Or Alfie. Or someone, anyhow.'

'Millie!' I scold her. 'You make it sound like any boy would do! You can't go kissing boys just for the sake of it!'

'It's not just for the sake of it. It's because it will be Valentine's Day, and I am thirteen, and I think I might be ready for a boyfriend.'

'Well, I'm not,' I say. 'And if I was, it would have to be someone special. It would have to be love.'

'What do you know about love?' Millie scoffs.

I think about a boy with dark wavy hair, a boy whose smile makes my heart do backflips, a boy who doesn't exist outside my imagination.

208

❀❀❀❀❀❀❀❀❀❀❀❀❀❀❀❀❀❀❀

'Nothing,' I say.

But I think I do.

It's a week since I went to the museum looking for clues and in that time nothing else has come up, but I am just packing up after history class when Mr Wolfe tells me that Grace, the museum lady, has found some old records that mention the gypsy farm workers. I bite my lip. Maybe, finally, there'll be some answers about Clara, and Finch.

Summer has an after-school dance class so I ask Coco to tell Mum I'll be home later and get off the school bus in Kitnor. Alfie Anderson falls into step beside me.

'Jobs to do in the big, bad city?' he asks, grinning.

'Kitnor isn't exactly big or bad,' I say. 'There is something I need to do, though.'

'Don't suppose it involves hot chocolate and marsh-mallows in the Mad Hatter with your favourite classmate, does it?' he asks hopefully.

'Millie got off two stops ago,' I shrug. 'So . . . no, not really.'

'I mean ME,' Alfie says, rolling his eyes.

'I know, I know,' I laugh. 'But no, I have to go to the

209

museum. I am trying to find out more about that old story about Clara Travers and the gypsy boy . . .'

'Cool,' Alfie says. 'It's ages since I've been to the museum.'

'You don't have to come,' I say. 'You might find it kind of boring.'

'No, I am getting into history a bit now,' he tells me. 'I won the quiz, didn't I? I might end up being one of those palaeo-wotsits Mr Wolfe was on about, the ones who dig up dinosaur bones!'

'Palaeontologists,' I supply.

'That's the ones. Anyway, I can look at fossils and old bones in the museum while you are doing whatever you need to do. And then we could go back to yours maybe, do some homework, watch a DVD, hang out . . .'

'Sorry,' I tell him. 'Summer won't be there – she has a ballet lesson in town.'

'I know that,' he says. 'She wasn't on the bus, and besides, I know her ballet timetable by heart. Maybe I just want to hang out with you, Skye!'

'Maybe you just want to pick my brains about Summer,' I correct him. 'Or else you'll just happen to be staying to tea when she gets home from dance class . . .'

'That's a great idea,' he says. 'It's Tuesday. Mum is making tofu and black bean casserole with shredded cabbage, and I'd kill for pizza and chips.'

'Too bad,' I grin, pushing open the museum door. I step into the shadowy interior, Alfie at my heels like an over-keen puppy. Grace looks up and grins. 'Skye!' she says. 'I was hoping you'd call in. I've copied out some names and dates from the parish register – Clara had two younger brothers, Charles and Robert, but both were killed in the Second World War. Kate Travers, your gran, was Robert's only daughter.'

'Right,' I say. 'So Clara was . . . what, my great-great-aunt?' It feels weird to put a name to it, but we're family, Clara and I – that must be why I feel such a connection to her.

'Exactly,' Grace agrees. 'I've also discovered some old farm records you might find interesting.'

She hands me an old ledger from Hazel Tree Farm, just down past the woods. The entries span the early 1920s, listing 'itinerant Romany workers' helping out with ploughing, planting, picking, harvest. It's pretty much the same ones turning up year after year. Sonny Brown, Dan

Cooper, Lucky Cooper, Sam Cooper, John Birch, Bobby Birch, Jack Sampson . . . there is no mention of the name Finch.

Maybe I invented the name as well as the boy?

Alfie stifles a yawn, but I ignore him.

'Skye, here's the entry I wanted you to see . . .'

The page is from February 1926, the black ink spidery and faded with age:

A great drama with the gypsies.

All winter they have been camped quietly in the woods, helping with hedge-laying and farm maintenence, mending pots and pans. Sometimes the women and children come to the village, selling clothes pegs or snowdrops, buying bread.

Today, in spite of the snow still thick upon the ground, all five wagons packed up abruptly and left the village. I questioned Dan Cooper as he led his piebald mare along the lane, and he claimed that Mr Travers at the big house had warned them off with threats and curses, telling them never to return to his land.

❀❀❀❀❀❀❀❀❀❀❀❀❀❀❀❀❀❀❀❀❀❀❀

'It was true then,' I say, my heart beating hard. 'Just like in the story.'

'Seems so,' Grace says. 'I do know that gypsies used to camp by the shoreline by Low Meadows Farm, right up until the 1970s. It may be they were the same families, and just changed their camping place, or they may have been a different lot completely . . . I'm not sure if we'll ever know for sure.'

'Thank you,' I say. 'This helps, anyway.'

'I'll let you know if I find anything else,' Grace says.

'What's the obsession with Clara and the gypsies?' Alfie wants to know as we head back out into the cold January afternoon. 'You know what happened. She was engaged to a toff, fell for a guy who ditched her, then chucked herself in the sea. What more is there to find out?'

I frown. 'The name of the gypsy boy,' I sigh. 'The date she died. I don't know, Alfie – details, proof, anything!'

'Why?' he asks. 'It won't change anything.'

Because I need to find out who Finch was, I think, but that's not something I can explain to Alfie.

Finch is real. I'm certain of it. He existed.

'I need to know,' I tell Alfie. 'I can't explain why . . . I just do. And if the museum can't help, where do I go to find out about people who lived and died all that time ago?'

We walk past the post office, and Alfie grins. 'How about Mrs Lee?' he suggests. 'She is always rattling on about how she's descended from the Romany gypsies. Maybe she really is?'

I stop in my tracks. 'You're a genius, Alfie! Come on!'

'What, now?' he argues. 'Skye, come on. Seriously, hot chocolate and marshmallows would be a much better option . . .'

He follows me anyway, hovering at my elbow.

'Skye!' Mrs Lee greets me. She sneaks a look at Alfie and raises one eyebrow knowingly. 'How are you? How's the romance going?'

'There is no romance,' I tell her. 'Not with Alfie. Definitely, absolutely not.'

'I'm not that bad, am I?' Alfie asks, hurt. 'You don't have to be quite so harsh about it.'

Mrs Lee picks up my palm, shaking her head. 'There is definitely something on your love line, Skye. No question about it. Love is in the air!'

'I seriously doubt it,' I say.

214

'Can you look at my palm?' Alfie says, opening his hand out on the counter. 'Because I think my love line might be looking quite lively too. I am almost certain of it.'

Mrs Lee studies his palm and nods thoughtfully. 'There is something,' she admits. 'But I'm seeing complications. Heartbreak and confusion. The course of true love never runs smooth.'

'You're kidding, right?' Alfie sulks. 'Because I don't actually want heartbreak and confusion, thank you. That sucks!'

'You did ask,' Mrs Lee shrugs. 'So, Skye, no post today?'

'Um . . . no. I was actually wondering . . . I am doing some research into the gypsy travellers who used to pass through Kitnor years ago. I know you've got traveller blood, and I wondered if maybe you knew anything . . .'

Mrs Lee narrows her eyes. 'Well, my mother was half-Romany, of course,' she says. 'Yes, she was born in a *vardo* – a bow-top wagon. It was a hard life but a wonderful one too . . . very free, in tune with nature, living close to the land. That way of life has all but vanished now . . . tarmac roads and cars made sure of that, and the way the farms were mechanized after the war. They didn't need casual labour any more.'

215

'I'd love to talk to your mum,' I say hopefully, but Mrs Lee shakes her head.

'Bless you, pet, but she died two or three years back now,' she says. 'My dad was a *gorja*, a non-Romany, and after a few years on the road they settled down in a village over Exeter way. I do have some old photographs you might like, though – I'll look them out for you.'

'Thanks. I don't suppose . . . it's a man named Finch I am trying to trace. You haven't heard of him at all?'

She frowns. 'I'm sorry, no,' she tells me. 'My mother was called Lin Cooper, Lin Martin after she married. I don't remember her mentioning a family called Finch. I do have some aunts and uncles still living, though, Lin's younger brothers and sisters. I could ask them.'

'Thank you,' I say. 'I appreciate that. Really.'

I buy a chocolate bar out of guilt and drag Alfie out of the shop.

'I don't think she has gypsy blood at all,' he huffs. 'She got my fortune completely wrong, because I am meant for Summer and it is only a matter of time before she realizes that . . .'

'If you say so,' I sigh, handing him a square of chocolate.

❀❀❀❀❀❀❀❀❀❀❀❀❀❀❀❀❀❀❀❀

'"Complicated",' she said,' he grumbles. 'Why does it have to be complicated? Just my luck. Not that I believe all that rubbish, obviously.'

'Obviously,' I say. 'I wonder if she'll remember to ask her aunts and uncles, or look for those old photos?' Although I'm not holding out much hope they'll give me the answers I need. It will probably turn out to be yet another dead end.

'What difference can a few photos make?' Alfie says. 'This is crazy, Skye. You know what happened. That story didn't have a happy ending – nothing you can do will change that. Let go of it. Live for the moment.'

He grabs my hat and runs off along the street with it, and I laugh and follow, our feet loud on the icy pavements, our breath trailing behind us like wisps of mist in the fading light.

28

On the first day of the half-term break, we wake up to a still, wintry world. The bare trees sparkle with icing-sugar snow and a thick blanket of white stretches over the garden and down towards the cliff path.

I look down from the window at Fred the dog running in crazy circles with Humbug at his heels, and Mum picking her way carefully down to feed the ducks, leaving a trail of perfect footprints behind her. Cherry is up too, muffled in a hat and scarf, breaking the ice on the fish pond so she can feed the goldfish.

I think of the gypsies packing up their woodland camp all those years ago, setting off along the snowy lanes in the middle of winter because Clara's father had driven them away in a fit of anger.

'This had better be gone by Thursday,' Summer says, appearing at my side. 'I don't mind snow, but why now? Why not last week, when we were at school? We might have got a few days off!'

'I know,' I say. 'Still, this way we get to enjoy it properly. It'll all be gone by Thursday, but if not, then it'll just make everything look even more magical. People will still come, Summer. Stop worrying!'

The bedroom door flies open and Coco runs in, dressed in about a dozen layers and wearing at least two scarves. 'Are you coming out for a snowball fight?' she grins. 'We could build a snowman too. Or an igloo! This is so cool!'

'Cool is the word,' Summer says, pulling on a jumper. 'I can't, Coco, I have ballet practice.'

'You always have ballet practice,' Coco huffs. 'You are worse than ever, lately. Don't you have time off for fun sometimes?'

'Ballet is fun,' Summer shrugs, pulling on leg warmers. 'And I'm too old for snowmen and igloos.'

'Skye?' my little sister appeals.

'Can it wait till later?' I ask. 'Millie is coming over, so we could all make a snowman . . .' I trail away into silence. 'On second thoughts, strike that. Millie won't want to. Let's just do it . . . get Cherry too, she's up already.'

'Yesss!' Coco says, punching the air. 'I don't see how anyone could ever be too old for snow!'

Mum has porridge on the go, and we wolf down big bowlfuls of it and bundle up and run outside, Fred the dog and Humbug the lamb trotting behind.

The three of us make a huge snowman right beside the fish pond, giving it pebble eyes and a carrot nose and one of Paddy's hats. We are in the middle of a snowball fight when Mum calls from the kitchen to tell me someone is on the phone for me.

'A boy,' she says, raising an eyebrow.

'A boy!' Coco squeals. 'Skye's got a boyfriend!'

'I haven't!' I growl. 'It's probably just Alfie.'

But Coco won't let go. 'Slush alert!' she teases. 'Skye and Alfie, sitting in a tree, K.I.S.S.I.N.G. . . .'

I grit my teeth and head into the kitchen, stomping the snow from my boots. Mum has been baking, and the rich aroma hangs in the air like a promise.

'Yes?' I say into the phone. 'What do you want, Alfie?'

'Your company,' he says brightly. 'I have a sledge and I

❀❀❀❀❀❀❀❀❀❀❀❀❀❀❀❀❀❀❀❀❀❀

am heading up to the hill beneath the woods, if you want to come? Um . . . anyone can come, obviously. Summer, or anyone. If they want to . . .'

I glance across at Summer, who is practising pliés with one hand on the kitchen dresser.

'They don't want to,' I say tiredly. 'Trust me.'

'I knew you were going to say that,' Alfie sighs. 'But you can't blame me for trying. Just you then, OK? It'll be fun, I promise. And we need to talk.'

'We are talking,' I point out.

'Talk properly,' he says. 'You know what I mean.'

Mum wafts a plate of golden, heart-shaped cookies under my nose, and I take one, still warm from the oven.

'Alfie, I am kind of busy today. Millie's coming over to try on her party outfit and test out some make-up ideas.'

'I'll bribe you with hot chocolate at the Mad Hatter,' he offers.

'Alfie . . .'

'Just say yes,' he pleads. 'Take pity on me. I need your help. Really.'

I take a bite of cookie and give Mum a thumbs-up as it melts on my tongue. 'I'll think about it.'

❁❁❁❁❁❁❁❁❁❁❁❁❁❁❁❁❁❁

'Meet you at the sledging field at three,' Alfie says briskly. 'Be there, Skye. Please?'

I give in. 'I suppose. It's a date.'

I hang up the phone and Coco unleashes a long wolf whistle.

'Skye's got a date!' she whoops. 'With Alfie Anderson!'

'It is not THAT kind of a date!' I protest.

'Leave Skye alone, Coco!' Mum says, laughing. 'And let me tell you about the phone call I had while you were all out in the snow! A woman called . . . what was it? Nikki Something-or-other. She works as a researcher for the BBC, and she'd seen the magazine feature about us, back before Christmas . . .'

Coco's eyes are huge. 'What did she want? Is she going to come and make a film of us? Are we going to be on the telly?'

'No, love,' Mum laughs again. 'She's researching for a period drama, and Kitnor is one of the locations she is looking into. She wanted to know about our gypsy caravan, she'd noticed it in the magazine pictures. Was it functional, did it still run, that kind of thing. She's bringing some of her team over in March to check it out, take some shots of the caravan and the area.

'They're going to stay here while they're researching too, so we'll have some real live TV people staying. And maybe they'll like the caravan . . . we'd get a fee for letting them use it, apparently, if they decide they want it for the actual series!'

'Wow,' Coco grins. 'The gypsy caravan might be famous!'

I think of a dream: bright caravans parked together in the woods, a fire blazing, music, laughter, and a beautiful boy who doesn't exist. I can't help smiling.

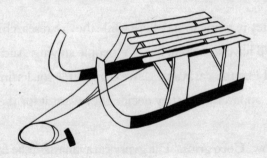

29

An hour watching Millie stare into my dressing-table mirror while testing out dozens of glittery eyeshadows and lipglosses has me so bored I am practically asleep.

'Does this look sort of retro?' she asks, half a false eyelash dangling from the corner of one eye. 'Vintage? It's very sixties, right?'

'Um . . . kind of,' I say.

'But will it clash with my dress?' she wonders out loud as the eyelash drops off and lands in her glass of Coke. 'Rats. I don't think I attached it right. I wish Summer was here – she knows about make-up.'

'She's at ballet,' I sigh. 'She's in a different class now. The times have changed.'

'I forgot,' Millie huffs. 'When will she be back?'

'Soon,' I say hopefully.

Not soon enough, I think.

'Want to take Fred out for a walk in the snow?' I suggest. 'Build an igloo maybe? Make snow angels?'

'I don't think so,' she says. 'I'm not exactly dressed for it. Isn't Honey here? Or Cherry? I didn't think it would just be us.'

'They're out,' I say. 'Coco's helping Paddy down in the workshop, though. I don't suppose you . . .'

'No way,' Millie says, piling her hair up on top of her head so that it looks like a demented pineapple. 'I'm cutting down on chocolate.'

Millie isn't cutting down on heart-shaped cookies, however. She has eaten at least six, in between telling me about the Valentine's cards she is planning to send, one to Alfie, one to Aaron and one to Sid. I stifle a yawn.

'Are you sending any?' she wants to know.

'No.'

Millie fixes me with a pitying look. 'It's OK, you know,' she says. 'Growing up is not a race. Some people can be

225

very mature at thirteen, and others aren't at all. You'll catch up, Skye.'

I blink. I think my best friend just called me immature.

My feet crunch through a thick crust of snow as I walk down to the village and along the lane to the sledging field, my face stinging from the cold. As I approach, I see a lone figure with an old wooden sledge plummeting down the hill towards me.

Alfie swerves his sledge to a halt beside me, spattering me with snow. 'You came!' he says. 'Cool! And only an hour late!'

'I had to wait until Millie went home – I told you,' I say. I don't tell him that I'd been counting the minutes until then. I feel bad just thinking it, but Millie's obsession with boys is starting to get to me, big style.

I look at Alfie and the seed of an idea takes hold – crazy but possibly brilliant.

'Listen, I have been thinking, Alfie. You probably have a lot in common with Millie. And she is quite pretty, really, have you noticed?'

'What are you trying to do?' Alfie growls. 'Set me up with Millie? I don't think so! My heart belongs to Summer.'

'OK, I am just saying. Millie is getting quite interested

❀❀❀❀❀❀❀❀❀❀❀❀❀❀❀❀❀❀❀❀

in boys,' I tell him. 'More than Summer, anyway. All she ever talks about is ballet. So maybe you should consider Millie? If you want to practise your kissing and stuff. I think she might quite like to kiss someone. She has been talking non-stop about boys and make-up and whether you can learn to kiss by snogging the inside of your elbow –'

'Can you?' Alfie asks, perking up. 'I didn't know that!'

'My best friend is full of tips like that, these days,' I say sadly. 'Seriously . . . I sometimes think the old Millie has been snatched by aliens.'

'You believe in aliens?' Alfie asks. 'Awesome! I do too! They could be watching us right now, and they have Millie, and they are planning which of us to capture next . . . how cool would that be?'

'I was joking, Alfie,' I say, and his face falls.

'I knew that,' he lies, jumping off the sledge to drag it back up the hill. 'Anyway . . . I do not fancy Millie, OK? I wanted to talk to you about the party. It'd take more than an alien abduction for me to miss out on that! Wait till you see what I'm wearing. I have a real vintage tailcoat! It used to be Dad's, but it is very cool, Victorian or something. Should I wear a trilby with it, or a top hat, do you think?'

❀❀❀❀❀❀❀❀❀❀❀❀❀❀❀❀❀❀❀❀❀

'Top hat, definitely,' I say, trudging after him up the slope.

'That's what I thought. I don't have one, though. I might have to settle for a beanie.'

'Too bad.'

'If Summer doesn't notice me in that tailcoat, she never will,' he says. 'I have a good feeling about this party, Skye. Things are going to change. I am going to prove Mrs Lee wrong – I don't see why my love life should have to be complicated. I'm changing tack. There will be no more secret Christmas cards and mystery presents. It's time to be upfront.'

'Do we have to go right up the hill?' I huff. 'I am getting frostbite here, I'm not joking.'

'You're not listening,' he frowns. 'This party is my big chance, Skye. It's Valentine's Day. I can't wait around forever for Summer to notice I exist. I have to show her that I am the perfect boy for her!'

'Alfie, are you sure about this?'

'Never surer.'

We finally reach the top of the hill and I flop down on the sledge to catch my breath.

'I have been wondering,' Alfie says. 'Why is Summer

called Summer when her birthday is in February? It doesn't make sense!'

'It does, kind of,' I say. 'Back when Mum and Dad were young and in love, and when Honey was just a tiny baby, they spent a long summer break on a Scottish island called Skye. And nine months later, we came along . . . they called us Summer and Skye.'

'Cool,' Alfie says. 'I like that story. I've got another question too. What IS Summer's perfect boy, exactly? What is she looking for in a boyfriend, do you think? What's her type?'

I sigh. 'Summer doesn't want a relationship,' I tell him. 'She's so hung up on ballet she doesn't have time for anything else. It's her dream, and trust me, it doesn't leave room for romance.'

'She looks awesome in a tutu,' he grins. 'I've got that picture from the Sunday paper's magazine up on my bedroom wall.'

'Too much information,' I tell him. 'Seriously, though, if you want to grab her attention you should probably enrol in dance classes and get yourself a pair of tights.'

'Not happening,' he says gruffly. 'No, I have decided. I

229

am going to stop mooning about and take the direct approach. I am going to ask her out.'

'Alfie –'

'I have to, Skye,' he insists. 'The way I figure it, she can either say yes or no. I have nothing to lose, right?'

'I guess,' I sigh. 'Alfie, I think my toes have frostbite. I thought you promised me hot chocolate?'

'Sledging first, hot chocolate second,' he says. 'Where is your sense of adventure? It hardly ever snows here. We can't waste it!'

'I haven't wasted it,' I tell him. 'I have built a snowman and had a snowball fight, and walked down to meet you. But I am freezing, and it's a long way down. I don't think I have ever been sledging. I am going off snow, seriously. Why don't we just leave it for . . . *yeeow!*'

Alfie shoves the sledge forward and jumps on behind me, and suddenly we are flying down the slope, skidding from side to side, at about a hundred miles an hour. I try to curl myself into a tiny ball, leaning back against Alfie whose legs are sticking out on either side.

'Hold tight!' he shouts into my ear.

I am screaming and Alfie is laughing and we're at the

✿✿✿✿✿✿✿✿✿✿✿✿✿✿✿✿✿✿✿✿✿✿✿

bottom of the hill and still going strong, and when I yell out to ask where the brakes are he just pulls on the rope at the front and puts his feet down in the snow. We skid and swerve and jolt and the sledge flips over, and I land face down with my mouth full of snow.

Everything hurts, and I have never been so cold in my whole, entire life. My cloche hat has vanished under a snowdrift and my hair feels like it is full of icicles. There is snow on my eyelashes and up my nose, snow slithering down my neck and melting icily inside my socks and gloves. I would cry, but the tears would freeze before they had a chance to fall.

Alfie rolls me over, leaning over me with an anxious expression. 'Skye?' he whispers. 'Skye? Speak to me!'

'You are in SO much trouble,' I mutter, spluttering snow everywhere.

Alfie grins. He hauls me up, and I stagger slightly, my teeth chattering. 'I'm sorry, I'm REALLY sorry. It went a lot faster with two of us on board. But hey, no broken bones!'

'There might be when I catch hold of you,' I say through gritted teeth.

He rescues my hat and empties out the snow, jamming it back on my head and carefully tucking a stray curl of snow-caked hair behind my ear. His fingers are surprisingly soft and warm against my cheek, and his eyes catch on to mine and hold for a long moment.

Alfie Anderson has the most amazing chocolate-brown eyes. Who knew?

His lips part a little as if he wants to say something and then thinks better of it, and I can see a little crease of confusion between his eyebrows. My heart beats a little harder and I realize his fingers are still warm against my cheek, which feels very strange but not entirely unpleasant.

And then I think of Finch, a ghost boy who only exists in my dreams. Finch makes my heart beat faster than Alfie ever could. I step back and Alfie takes his hand away, uncertainly, brushing the snow from his jeans and jacket. The moment is lost.

I blink.

Falling for a girl who has an identical twin sister must be kind of strange. Complicated, as Mrs Lee would say.

I know something, though. My days of being second

best are over, and I won't settle for a second-best boy either. It might sound crazy, but a dream boy is better than the wrong boy . . .

30

I always thought that having a birthday on Valentine's Day was pretty cool, but I guess I didn't think it through. I did not predict the ways it could go wrong now Summer and I are teenagers, or that three cartoon Valentine's cards addressed to my twin could actually hurt so much.

'Three!' she says, cheeks pink with pleasure. 'Wow!'

'Great,' I say flatly. 'Awesome.'

'Oh, I think there's one for you!' she says. 'Look!'

I open the pale blue envelope hopefully, but it's just a birthday card from Mum's cousin Lucy, who always sends us a card each even though most people send a shared one.

My heart sinks. Will it be like this every year from now on? Will I end up hating my own birthday?

We have never had Valentine's cards before, unless you

count the heart-shaped toast and jam Mum always makes or a very sticky Love Hearts sweet Alfie gave me in Year Three, and it said *Crazy* so I don't. Besides, he gave Summer the rest of the packet, now that I think back.

Not getting a Valentine has never mattered before, but today, with Summer mooning over her cards, it does. I knew she'd have one from Alfie, of course, but three . . . that seems kind of hard to take. Three boys are crushing on my twin sister, and nobody at all fancies me. That's harsh.

We look exactly alike, so what is it that makes her special? Boys fancy her, adults are entranced by her, friends flutter around her like moths drawn to a flame. I don't even blame them. Summer was born to be in the spotlight. I seem destined for the shadows.

'You can have one of my Valentines,' Summer says brightly, and suddenly I have to blink back the tears, even though it's only breakfast time and today is my birthday and there's a big party to look forward to later on. I should be the happiest girl alive.

But I didn't actually want a party, and I really, really do not want one of Summer's cast-off Valentine's cards. It feels like rubbing salt in the wound. I take a bite of heart-shaped

❀ ❀ ❀ ❀ ❀ ❀ ❀ ❀ ❀ ❀ ❀ ❀ ❀ ❀ ❀ ❀ ❀ ❀ ❀ ❀

toast and jam, but it tastes like sawdust. Summer pushes her plate away too, untouched.

'Not hungry, you two?' Mum asks. 'Come on, birthday girls, I made that specially!'

'Can't,' Summer says. 'I'm too excited to eat!'

'Me too,' I say, but it's not excitement, it's dread.

I fix a smile on my face, a wide, bright smile that hides the sad, sour feeling inside. I don't know what is wrong with me. I should be happy for Summer, not envious. The only Valentine I really want would come from Finch, a boy with dark wavy hair and a smile that makes my heart do somersaults . . . and that's impossible, of course.

We open our presents. There is a pinboard collage made from twelve little snapshots of Summer and me, each one taken on past birthdays, stretching from last year, when we turned twelve, right back to when we were tiny. Twelve pictures of Summer and me, laughing, holding hands, and a space for one more photo, a photo from today.

'Gorgeous,' Summer says, grinning. 'How cute?'

But pictures of how happy we were back then just underlines the fact that things have changed.

In the photo from when we were ten, we are side by side,

but Summer is facing into the sun and I am half in shadow. In the next year's photo we seem to be holding hands, but when I look more closely I can see that Summer is actually gripping my arm, as if I might run away. The year after, we are barely touching at all.

Tears sting my eyes again and I brush them away quickly, before anyone can see.

The next present is matching mobile phones, a pink one for Summer, a blue one for me; then a cream lace minidress with a twenties vibe for Summer and a longer, more authentic version for me.

'It was Summer's idea. She picked it out,' Mum says hopefully. 'We all thought it had a really vintage look. Do you like it, Skye?'

'It's lovely,' I say truthfully. 'Thank you!'

But a part of me thinks that Summer has picked it out so that we can look more obviously like twins in our almost-matching dresses; so that I won't wear one of Clara's velvet frocks. I didn't want a new dress, I didn't want a party . . . but I have them anyway, and it seems ungrateful to complain.

Grandma Kate sends us another charm each for our

❀❀❀❀❀❀❀❀❀❀❀❀❀❀❀❀❀❀❀❀❀❀

bracelets, two silver heart shapes to signify that our birthday is on Valentine's Day.

A photo collage, matching mobiles, matching charms, almost-matching dresses . . . I thought it was cute, once, to have the same presents as Summer. These days it just seems like another way for people to forget that we're individuals, for me to fade a little next to Summer's vivid charm.

'One last thing,' Paddy says, handing a small, ribbon-wrapped box to me and one to Summer. 'I was doing some experiments and I came up with a couple of new truffle ideas specially for you two . . .'

My little box contains a cache of milk chocolate truffles, heart-shaped and iced with a spidery icing-sugar snowflake. I bite into one. The sweet, soft taste of marshmallow melts on to my tongue, all vanilla and sugar and molten stickiness. It takes my breath away. Suddenly the sad, heavy feeling doesn't seem quite as bad as before.

'Paddy, that is amazing,' I say with feeling. 'I mean, honestly, that is the best thing I have ever tasted. I love marshmallow, obviously, but that . . . that's something else!'

'It's my own recipe,' he says. 'Marshmallows were originally made from marshmallow root sweetened with rose

✿✿✿✿✿✿✿✿✿✿✿✿✿✿✿✿✿✿✿✿✿

water and honey – it's one of the oldest sweet treats we have, did you know that? I've been trying out old recipes, experimenting a bit. Using real marshmallow root and rose water makes such a difference . . .'

'It makes one amazing truffle flavour!' I grin.

'I've called it Marshmallow Skye in your honour, and the other one is Summer's Dream, which is strawberry themed because that's Summer's favourite, or so I'm told . . .'

'Can I taste?' I ask, and Summer offers me one of her chocolates, white and heart-shaped and drizzled with pink, the centre a dreamy confection of strawberries and cream. 'Oh . . . that's gorgeous too!'

'Thanks, Paddy,' Summer says. 'I love this, but I'm saving mine until later! I'm so excited right now I couldn't eat a thing!'

Later, Paddy drives us down to the village hall.

'Everyone's so excited about the party!' Summer says. 'People have been texting me all morning, I have no idea how I survived so long without a mobile!'

'Great,' I say listlessly.

I spend the afternoon with Paddy, Cherry and Summer, hanging home-made heart-shaped bunting and endless

239

strings of fairy lights and handpainted birthday banners all around the hall. Summer glows with excitement while I struggle to keep a smile on my face. My whole body feels slow, heavy, unwilling.

Mum comes down with the food and we set out plates of my favourite marshmallow cupcakes and mountains of truffles dredged with snowy icing-sugar drifts. There are trays of heart-shaped mini pizzas and sausage rolls to be warmed up in the hall's little kitchen, and bowls of crisps and dips and the most beautiful heart-shaped chocolate birthday cake. Paddy sets up the drinks and Shay arrives to test out the sound equipment and run through some of his playlist.

Even I have to smile as the hall comes to life, shimmering under the fairy lights as the daylight fades, the food piled up like a picture in a magazine, music curling around us as we make the finishing touches to our decorations.

'Now will you believe it's going to be cool?' Summer says to me.

I almost think she's right.

31

Summer is wearing her new dress, her hair pinned up and twisted into golden ringlets with a 1920s headband made from pink ribbon with Alfie's flower attached. She looks amazing. Me, I am wearing the green velvet flapper dress layered over white petticoats. I am huddled into the emerald-green coat and still I cannot get warm.

'Skye!' my twin exclaims when she sees me. 'I thought . . . I wanted us to look alike!'

'We look alike no matter what we wear,' I tell her reasonably. 'I love the new dress, Summer, but this is what I planned to wear. I don't want us to look like little kids in matching outfits, and besides, I'm freezing – I'll shiver all night if I wear that. Another time, I promise.'

❀❀❀❀❀❀❀❀❀❀❀❀❀❀❀❀❀❀❀

'But you're wearing the green dress,' she states. 'And the coat, the things from my dream. My nightmare. You know how I feel about them, Skye.'

'It's not about you, Summer,' I say quietly. 'It's my birthday. I can wear what I like, surely?'

Summer bites her lip, and if Mum and Paddy are hurt that I'm not wearing the birthday dress they don't say. We pile into Paddy's minivan.

'It's freezing,' I whisper, as he drives carefully down the hill. 'Is this a new Ice Age or something?'

'It's going to snow again,' Coco grins. 'It's SO exciting!'

The hall is lit up in the darkness and I can hear the thump of music from inside as we pile out. One perfect snowflake drifts down on to my coat sleeve, and then another, and suddenly we are looking up at the ink-black sky and it looks like someone has shaken out a feather pillow, with tiny white flakes drifting softly down.

'It's beautiful!' I gasp, and I wish I could stay out here in the darkness with the feathery snowflakes swirling all around me.

Paddy goes ahead of us into the hall, and suddenly the music cuts off and the lights die. Coco is laughing.

'They're doing it like a surprise party,' she warns us. 'As if you don't know what's going on!'

Summer goes in and Cherry and Coco steer me after her, as if I might run away without their hands guiding me. Inside, the hall is still and dark. My eyes decipher the shadow-shapes of people, my ears detect tiny whispers, shuffles and stifled giggles.

And then the sounds system erupts with 'Happy Birthday' and the lights blaze bright and everyone is singing and yelling and Summer and I are pulled into the middle of it all, party poppers exploding all around us, moving from hug to hug.

Shay has the perfect playlist, a mix of dance tunes and cheesy retro stuff that makes everyone laugh. The dance floor is full and everyone has made an effort with the Vintage Valentine theme, even if it's just an old trilby hat for the boys or a shawl or flower in the hair for the girls.

Cherry is with her new high-school friends, Coco with her crazy mates, and Honey is turning heads in a blue satin slip-dress and the feathered headband from Clara's trunk. She has a geeky, serious boy in tow, a boy who looks a little like the non-Superman version of Clark Kent but without the broad shoulders and manly jaw.

243

❀❀❀❀❀❀❀❀❀❀❀❀❀❀❀❀❀❀❀❀❀❀

'Honey's new friend,' Mum tells me, eyes wide. 'Anthony. He's helping her with her maths and science! Looks like she is starting to listen to us at last . . .'

Cherry says Anthony is a Year Ten boy from the high school who is super-smart and swotty and some kind of computer whizz.

'He's not her usual type,' I say.

Cherry shrugs. 'Maybe she's changed,'

Or not. Maybe Honey has just dragged Anthony along so we'll think that. Later on I see him talking to Mum about revision notes and study methods, while in the opposite corner Honey is holding court to a crowd of high-school boys and drinking cider straight from the bottle.

Millie, in her faux 1960s boho dress and glittery eyeshadow and spidery false lashes drags me up to dance to every song, wiggling her hips a lot, and fluttering her lashes at any boy who comes near. 'This is amazing!' she yells into my ear, above the beat of the music.

It's kind of amazing, but my head is starting to hurt from the thumping bass and I'm hot and tired and achey from dancing. 'I need a drink,' I tell Millie, and slip away though the crowd of dancers.

❀❀❀❀❀❀❀❀❀❀❀❀❀❀❀❀❀❀❀❀

Alfie grabs my elbow, bright-eyed and hopeful in his vintage tailcoat. He looks a million miles away from the annoying clown with the wind-tunnel hair of just a few months back. I think that if my sister really looked at him, she would see that he is actually quite cute, but I don't think Alfie Anderson is on Summer's radar at all.

She is in the middle of the dance floor, in the centre of a big knot of boys and girls, her blonde hair flying out around her as she moves to the music. She looks happier than I have ever seen her.

'I'm getting a drink,' I shout above the music, and Alfie grins and tows me through the crowd to the drinks table, collecting two paper cups of lemonade.

'Thanks,' I tell him. 'I'm not feeling good . . . so hot . . . and thirsty.'

He steers me towards the door, and we escape from the crush and the racket into cool, perfect, white-out. The snow is falling steadily, muffling everything, covering up any remnants of grey slush and draping the parked cars in a thick cloak of white.

I raise my face, trying to catch snowflakes on my tongue.
'Are you OK?' Alfie asks.

❀❀❀❀❀❀❀❀❀❀❀❀❀❀❀❀❀❀❀❀❀

'Mmm . . . it's just so hot in there. My head feels like someone filled it with cotton wool and then hit it hard with a baseball bat.'

He frowns. 'I don't think you're well,' he says. He puts a hand out to my cheek and holds it there, and I notice how cool his fingers are against my burning skin.

'You're boiling,' he says. 'Remember the flu bug? I think we should tell your mum.'

'It's just the dancing, seriously,' I argue. 'I'm fine.' I scoop up a handful of snow and press it against my cheeks, and a delicious shiver runs through my body as it melts.

'Are you sure?'

'Sure.'

'So,' Alfie says. 'I am going to do it. I really, really am. I am going to ask Summer to dance, and then I am going to ask her out. Wish me luck!'

'Good luck, Alfie!'

He runs a hand through his hair, straightens his tailcoat and squares his shoulders. 'Um . . . so . . . now, do you think?' he asks.

'Go for it.'

I follow him inside, watching as he walks along the edge

of the dancers, chin tilted, determined. And then I see his shoulders droop, his face crease with confusion in the flickering light, and I follow his gaze.

Summer is slow-dancing with Aaron Jones, her arms looped round his neck, her head on his shoulder. Aaron's face shines as if he has just won the lottery, and as I watch he pulls her closer still and buries his face in her hair.

A jolt of pain stabs through me. I'd love to slow-dance with a boy, to feel his arms round me, his face in my hair, but only if that boy were Finch. I want something I can never have.

I should be happy for my sister. I should be, but I just feel sad and small and left behind, the shadow twin.

What must Alfie be feeling?

But when I turn round I can't see him.

I turn away from the dance floor and ditch my paper cup, pick up a paper plate and fight my way over to the food.

'Everything OK, Skye?' Mum shouts above the music. 'Having a good time?'

'Brilliant!' I bite into a sausage roll but it tastes like cardboard, and the crisps stick in my throat like glass. I want to be somewhere else, anywhere else but here.

Summer said I was obsessed with the past, living in a dream world. Maybe she was right. I like my dream world a whole lot better than this one. The past is a shadowy place, a dark place, sweet and sticky as marshmallow. It's an easy place to hide. I stand there on the outskirts of the party, wishing I could escape.

'Unreal,' Coco yells in my ear a few minutes later. 'I mean, kind of gross, really. And I always thought it was you he liked!'

'What?' I frown.

'You know,' she yells through the racket. 'Alfie. And Millie. Kissing. Seriously, how can he do that?'

I look where Coco is pointing and see that my matchmaking has paid off after all. Millie has her arms clamped round Alfie, her lips suctioned on to his.

'Are you OK, Skye? You look kind of wobbly . . .'

'I'm fine,' I say, but Coco is right. I feel unsteady, as if my legs might give way, as if I might cry. I should be pleased for Alfie and Millie, but I'm not – I feel more lost, more alone than ever.

Summer is coming towards me through the crowd, Aaron trailing behind. 'Hey!' she yells above the music. 'Have you

❁❁❁❁❁❁❁❁❁❁❁❁❁❁❁❁❁❁❁❁❁

seen Millie and Alfie? Looks like you missed your chance there! They make a good couple, though. Alfie is not exactly cool, is he? And Millie tries hard, but what's she done to her make-up? Are those false lashes? They look like spiders stuck to her eyelids!'

I shut my eyes for a second and the room seems to spin.

Loyalty to Alfie and Millie swamps me, and the hurt and confusion they have caused me over the past few months evaporates. In a couple of careless sentences, Summer has dismissed my friends completely. Alfie, who has been crushing on her forever; Millie, who hero-worships her. The two best friends I have, although they have a million faults, of course . . . to Summer, they are barely visible.

I want to answer Summer, to tell her that not everyone can be as cool as she is, not everyone can be a star, but she has moved on already, tugging Aaron along in her wake.

I wonder if Alfie was right, if I am actually ill instead of sick with anger and self-pity. I elbow my way through the dancers, heading for the door, and when I catch sight of Summer feeding heart-shaped pizza to Aaron Jones I feel even worse.

I do not want to be here. I want a world where the sun

❀❀❀❀❀❀❀❀❀❀❀❀❀❀❀❀❀❀❀

shines, where the air smells of woodsmoke and a boy with laughing eyes puts wildflowers in my hair and whirls me round and round beneath the trees until the two of us are breathless.

And then I see him, through the crowd, a face in the doorway, a boy I have never seen before except in my dreams, a boy with suntanned skin and dark, wavy hair and a grin that takes all the broken pieces of my heart and puts them back together again as good as new.

Finch.

32

I move through the crowd, not thinking about what I will say, not wondering why or how he is here, just glad that he is. I glimpse his face again as he turns away, the door closing behind him.

When I get outside he has gone, and I think I might cry. Then I see a lone figure in the darkness, picking his way through the snow, and I run inside and grab my coat because I understand now. Loud music and hot, sweaty crowds of kids are not the place for Finch and me to meet. That's not the way I dreamt it.

I pull the emerald-green coat close around me, my feet slipping and sliding in the snow as I hurry along. I follow the shadowy figure along the road to the edge of the village, up the lane that leads towards the woods. I frown, because

I cannot see his footprints, which must mean the snow is falling faster than I think.

When I see him climb the stile and move into the woods I follow, although my fingers shake as I hang on to the slippery wood and I lose my footing on the other side and fall down in the snow.

I don't even care. The icy shock of it cools my burning skin.

I scramble to my feet, struggling up the hill, picking my way through the little, twisty trees, their branches bent low with the weight of white. I cannot see him now, but I keep going, my shoes full of snow, feet frozen, breathless, hands pushing back the branches that reach out to scratch me as I pass.

And then, too late, I realize I am alone in the woods, in the dark, and that the boy I was following has gone, was probably never there at all. I try to call out, but no sound comes and a stab of pain lodges in my throat when I try to swallow back the disappointment.

I am shivering, huge, rippling shudders that slide through my whole body, yet my face is burning still.

'Finch?' I whisper, and the tears come then, sliding down

my pink cheeks like ice. I am ill, my head thumping, my limbs numb and heavy as if I have been swimming for hours through icy water and still cannot see the shore. I can't go on, and even though I know I mustn't, know it is the worst thing possible to do, I crouch down in the snow, pull Clara's coat around me, rest my head on my knees.

Somewhere in the distance I can hear my twin's voice calling me. For a moment I feel like I am in Summer's nightmare, a girl drowning, struggling for breath, fighting to stay afloat . . . and then the water closes over my head and I let the world drift away.

The scent of marshmallow and woodsmoke drifts across my senses and the sound of birdsong lifts me from sleep. I don't know whether a minute or an hour has gone by, but when I open my eyes the woods are green again, and although that's really not possible I don't question it at all. It's daylight and the pain and fever have gone, and inside my clasped hands I feel a warm, soft fluttering of feathers.

I open my palms wide, and huddled there I see a tiny bird, head grey, wings brown, breast flushed with pink. There's the softest of scratching as it scrabbles around on

❀❀❀❀❀❀❀❀❀❀❀❀❀❀❀❀❀❀❀❀

my palms, softer than silk, warm and fragile and perfectly tame.

I dredge up a memory. *A tame linnet in a powder-blue cage . . .*

'You're free,' I whisper. 'We're both free, now.'

The little bird blinks and shivers and I lift my cupped palms and as I do I notice the gold band on the third finger of my left hand, feel the weight of the ring, see the glint of the diamond. Then the bird spreads its wings and flies, a swift flash of brown wings and forked tail, fluttering up through the canopy of leaves and soaring beyond.

I watch until it is no more than a speck against the marshmallow clouds above.

Then I take off the engagement ring and push it deep into the pocket of the emerald-green coat, and my heart feels light and free, the way the linnet must have felt stretching its wings to fly free at last.

As the bird rises up, I seem to rise too, until I am up above the treetops, looking down at the girl below, a girl with red-gold hair cut into a swinging 1920s bob, blush-pink mallow flowers tucked behind her ear. She shrugs off the green coat, unwanted, a reminder of a life she no longer wants or needs. There is a crunching of twigs, a rustle of leaves, and I see a boy walk towards the girl, dark-skinned, smiling. He pulls her close and kisses her, and somewhere in my mind I understand that he is not the boy from my dreams but an older boy – a young man. But that doesn't matter at all because the girl is not me but Clara, and everything is finally right.

'I love you,' a voice whispers, and I can't tell whether it's inside my head or down below me. 'Always.'

When I wake again all of that has gone, and I am curled in the snow, so cold the hem of my dress is frosted with white and there are snowflakes on my eyelashes, my lips, my fingers.

I struggle to hang on to the memory of the linnet and the gypsy boy and the ring, but it slides away as if it never happened at all. I know I have to remember, though. I know it is important. I slip my shaking fingers into the pocket of the coat. It is empty, as always.

But just then my fingers snag against a tear in the lining. The pocket gives way and finally, right down inside the lining, I find them.

A ring, a letter.

I pull them out, my teeth chattering, hands trembling. I

try to focus, to read, but everything blurs and all I can do is hold the ring and the letter close, the breath rattling in my chest, eyes closing even as the voices drift up through the trees towards me, voices calling my name.

33

The room is dark, and sometimes when I wake the doctor is here, his stethoscope cold and shivery, and sometimes it is Mum, offering me sips of water to help me swallow down my tablets, wiping my face with a cool flannel. Often, though, it is Summer who stays with me, stroking my damp hair, holding my hand.

The doctor is talking to Mum and Paddy in a hushed voice about breaking the fever, about what would happen if the antibiotics don't work and they have to take me to hospital.

'I'm scared,' Mum says, and Paddy tells her to be strong, for me.

The clock ticks on endlessly, painful, louder than my heartbeat.

Summer is here again, telling me to come back because she needs me, she can't be without me, I am the other half of her.

'Stay,' she whispers, in the middle of the night when my dreams pull me backwards to another time and place. 'Stay with me, Skye, please?'

But the dreams are too strong. When I close my eyes a kaleidoscope of images crowd in unbidden, a jumble of snapshot memories from a life I never lived, jigsaw pieces that make no sense and can never be fitted together.

A gypsy caravan, a smiling girl with wildflowers in her hair, a young man in the firelight, a toddler with fluffy curls, a piebald horse, a skinny dog chasing rabbits, a blue sky with a linnet swooping and soaring, birdsong, laughter. The dream girl puts an arm round me, offers me a hot, sweet tea that tastes of marshmallow and honey. 'It's healing,' she whispers, and I swallow down the thick brew obediently although my throat feels like it is full of knives.

Another voice drifts across my sleep.

'Come back,' my twin whispers. 'I need you . . .'

But I am lost in dreams.

*

'You found her ring,' Summer tells me, hours, maybe days, later. 'Was it in the coat? And her letter. You solved the mystery, Skye, do you remember?'

My eyes flicker open. 'I did?'

And Summer reads to me, but the words are Clara's and as I listen the pain in my chest softens and lifts away.

'I am sorry, Harry, so sorry,' she reads. *'I thought I loved you, but I was too young, in love with the idea of love. By the time I realized, it was too late. I was trapped, like the linnet in its cage, afraid to disappoint you . . . and then I met Sam. He is not rich, like you, or from a well-connected family. He is as different from you, Harry, as night is from day. But I love him, and I am so, so, sorry for that because there is no way out of the mess I have made without hurting you, and that was never what I wanted, I promise . . .'*

Summer strokes my hair. 'Shall I go on?' she asks, and I open my eyes and nod my head and the rest of the story spills out, into the open where it should have been all these years.

'Father found out about Sam three months ago and sent him and his family away, telling me that I must forget him and go ahead with our wedding as planned. It was my duty, Father said. But as the weeks and months went by I knew that I could not marry you, Harry. I could

not deceive you. Sam sent a message to me and we agreed to run away together, to marry and give the baby I am expecting a home and a family bound by love. I could not trick you, you see. I could not marry you and ask you to raise another man's child, even to save myself and my family from shame.

'I am leaving you this letter and my engagement ring, and I have let the linnet fly free as all wild birds should. Perhaps in time you will come to forgive me, although I fear that Father and Mother never will. Do not be afraid for me. I am with Sam and I am happy, and I hope one day you will find it in your heart to understand.

Yours with true regard always,

Clara Jane Travers

May 31st 1926.'

Summer squeezes my hand. 'Do you see, Skye?' she whispers. 'It's not a suicide note. Clara didn't drown. She really did run away.'

My forehead creases. 'I don't understand . . . the stories . . . why?'

Summer shrugs. 'To save the family name?' she says. 'To spare Harry the truth, make sure the villagers never knew about the scandal of a rich man's daughter who got pregnant out of wedlock and ran away with the gypsies? They covered it all up, hid away her things, invented a story so sad and so shocking that nobody ever dared challenge it. Things were different then, Skye.'

My eyes well with tears, and Summer wipes them gently away.

'You've been miles away, these last few months,' she whispers. 'In some sort of dream world. I never thought I could be so jealous of a box of velvet dresses! And now all this . . . it's spooky. Like it was all meant to happen, so you'd find the letter, so the truth would come out . . .'

'It was meant,' I say softly. 'I know it was.'

'Maybe,' Summer says. 'But you've had us all so scared. These last few days . . . and before that too. I don't know why . . . I just knew something bad was going to happen.'

'But nothing bad has happened,' I point out. 'I'm OK. And now we have the letter, and we know the truth . . . there's nothing to be scared of any more. I can't believe I had the answers all the time – hidden in the coat you hated so much.'

I manage a faint smile. And I wonder how much of the conflict between Summer and me has been because of this, because she was trying, all along, to protect me? The more she tried, the more I pulled away from her, and the secrets piled up between us, pushing us further and further apart.

'You're stronger than I am, Skye, you always have been,' my twin sighs. 'I need you. You know that, right?'

I think of the photographs on our birthday collage, of light and dark, sunshine and shadow, of me ready to run, Summer hanging on to me. I thought it was to hold me back, but perhaps she is right, and it was just because she needs me?

'We need each other,' I whisper. 'But sometimes, Summer . . . well, you have to let go. We'll always need each other, but we need our freedom too.'

'I've been stupid,' Summer says. 'Stressed out. Selfish. Jealous too . . . of how close you are with Cherry, with Alfie. The way you can stand up to Honey and actually get through to her while I'm still treading on eggshells, scared to upset her. Things are changing, aren't they? We're changing. We used to do everything together, think the same, feel the same . . .'

'Did we?' I ask. 'Maybe once . . . a very long time ago. Not for a while now.'

❀❀❀❀❀❀❀❀❀❀❀❀❀❀❀❀❀❀❀❀

Summer rakes a hand through her long hair. 'Oh, God . . . I'm sorry, Skye. I've really messed up.'

'We both have,' I say. 'But so what? We can fix it. Change isn't always bad.'

We have a lot of sorting out to do, my twin and I. We need to talk, more honestly than we ever have, and there will be no more room for secrets or lies. I think of my marshmallow dream world, of Summer's dislike for all things sweet and sticky.

'You don't think I'm plain and boring and nothingy then?' I ask, and Summer's eyes widen as if I am crazy.

'Plain?' she echoes. 'Boring? Are you kidding me, Skye? Trust me, you're the least "nothingy" person I know! You're cool and creative and soft and sweet and kind . . .'

I let the fears drift away. I think we can do it. Somehow, over the coming weeks and months we will find a way to stay close without anyone having to stay in the shadows or anyone feeling second best. We will both have to work out how to let go a little, unpick the little jealousies, spread our wings, learn to trust. I'm pretty sure we can do it.

Summer isn't perfect, but I don't need her to be. I just need her to love me.

❀❀❀❀❀❀❀❀❀❀❀❀❀❀❀❀❀❀❀❀

She curls up beside me, her cool hand wrapped tightly round mine, the way it always used to be. 'We never do this any more,' I whisper. 'Hold hands.'

'I'm always holding your hand, Skye,' Summer says softly into the darkness. 'Whether you know it or not. I always will.'

I close my eyes, and this time no dreams crowd in to torment me.

The fever breaks and the doctor says I am well enough to have visitors. Cherry brings me jasmine tea in a tiny china cup and Coco smuggles Humbug up to see me and plays a long, creaking solo on the violin that almost makes me wish I was still curled up in a snowdrift. Honey paints me in watercolours, pale and waif-like with smudges of blue beneath my eyes.

Millie turns up with flowers and rebukes. 'You frightened us all to death, Skye. Once we realized you were missing from the party the place went crazy, seriously. What was all that about?'

'I think I was delirious,' I say.

'If Summer hadn't found you, lying in the snow . . .'

'I know,' I sigh. 'But she did.' And my heart-to-heart with Summer inspires me to be honest with Millie now.

'Millie,' I say carefully. 'We've been best friends for a long time, haven't we?'

'Ages,' she agrees. 'Since forever.'

'And . . . do you think we'll carry on being best friends? Because sometimes I feel like we are drifting apart, and I know that everyone changes a little as they get older, but . . . well, things seem a bit shaky right now. I hate it.'

'I'm not very good at being a teenager,' she says in a small voice, and when I look up I see that her cheeks are pink and her eyes are misty.

'What do you mean?'

Millie bites her lip. 'It's just – I'm no good at it,' she repeats. 'I didn't think any boy would ever really like me, until Alfie at the party. I'm not even sure he's all that keen, really. Boys never notice I'm around, and I never know if I'm getting the fashion thing right at all. It's all right for you, Skye.

'I'm not like you. I'm just ordinary. You're not, and you never will be – people notice you because you're pretty and friendly and kind and you wear all that cool vintage stuff, and I know I moan about it sometimes but the truth is you always look great, and I'm jealous of that. I tried borrowing some of your stuff, remember, last year? I looked like I was going to a fancy-dress party. A really bad one.'

'Oh, Millie,' I sigh. 'I thought you were fed up with me. I thought I was losing you.'

'I thought the same about you!' she says.

'I thought you were dumping me for Summer!'

Millie's shoulders droop. 'Summer's brilliant,' she says. 'I'd love a sister like that. But you – you're my best friend!'

Relief floods through me and I don't care any more about Millie's crushes and her crazes and her snippy words because best friends can forgive each other anything.

'You're right – I am. Best friends forever.' I manage to give her a weak hug.

'So . . .' I grin. 'Are you going out with Alfie now?'

Millie frowns. 'Maybe,' she says. 'We must be, right? He is playing it cool, but he seemed to be interested, at the party. I think we make a great couple!'

'Sure,' I say. 'I expect you do.'

Alfie turns up soon after Millie leaves, with a packet of marshmallows, half-eaten. 'I didn't mean to,' he says guiltily.

❀❀❀❀❀❀❀❀❀❀❀❀❀❀❀❀❀❀❀❀❀

'I was just testing them, but they're sort of addictive.' I guess it is the thought that counts.

'I hear you have a new girlfriend,' I say.

'You hear wrong,' Alfie huffs. 'Did Millie say that?'

'Let's just say she's hoping . . .'

Alfie shakes his head. 'I am in love with Summer,' he says, lowering his voice and glancing awkwardly over his shoulder in case my twin is lurking somewhere. 'And I am a one-girl kind of boy.'

'I noticed,' I say.

'Millie grabbed me!' he argues. 'I swear, I didn't stand a chance. She is a man-eater!'

'Who knew?' I laugh.

The next day, when I am properly on the mend, Mrs Lee comes to visit with a brown envelope full of photographs. 'I promised I'd look out Mum's pictures of the old days,' she says. 'The Romanies, the travellers. And then I heard you were ill, and I thought I'd call in.'

'Oh!' I blink. 'Thank you!'

She spreads the photos across my quilt, a patchwork of black-and-white images from the past, and as I look my heart begins to beat faster. I have never seen these pictures before. The people in them must be long gone . . . and yet they look familiar.

A young woman with mallow flowers in her hair, a man with dark skin creased with smiles, a toddler with dark fluffy curls . . . groups of children with muddied knees and Sunday-best clothes, bow-top wagons, piebald horses, camp fires. There are later snapshots of a young woman in a 1950s dress, an older couple smiling at the camera, sitting on the steps of a bow-top wagon. Just like my dreams.

'Who are these people?' I whisper.

'This was my mum, Lin,' Mrs Lee explains, pointing at the toddler with the fluffy curls. 'And her parents. Here's a later one of her, after she met my dad, and one of my grandparents with their *vardo*. They travelled all over Somerset and beyond in those days, but times got harder for the Romanies after the war . . . my mum lived in a house once she was married. Even my grandparents had a council house towards the end. They never forgot the old ways, though.'

I pick up the photograph of the middle-aged couple on the caravan steps, an earlier one of the same man smiling, the young woman with mallow flowers in her hair.

❀❀❀❀❀❀❀❀❀❀❀❀❀❀❀❀❀❀❀❀❀

'What were their names?' I ask. 'Your grandparents?'

Mrs Lee smiles softly. 'Sam Cooper, my grandad was called,' she says. 'And Jane.'

Jane . . . A jigsaw piece falls into place. Clara Jane Travers . . . who ran away and reinvented herself as Mrs Jane Cooper. I am looking at a ghost, and my eyes brim with tears.

I have worn her dresses, played her music, felt the rich scent of her marshmallow-sweet perfume drift around me. I have even dreamt her dreams, her memories, or something very close to that. And now at last her story has unfolded.

Clara Travers. She lived, and she loved, and she was happy . . . and she ended her days in a council house near Exeter with the man she adored. Happy endings don't get any better than this.

'And what was your mum's name again?' I ask, thinking of Clara's last letter to Harry, the baby she was carrying, Sam Cooper's baby.

Mrs Lee picks up the photo of the fluffy-haired toddler. 'Lin,' she tells me. 'Short for Linnet. It's a woodland bird, a kind of finch . . . very rare now. A beautiful name, don't you think?'

❀❀❀❀❀❀❀❀❀❀❀❀❀❀❀❀❀❀❀❀❀❀

I think of a small brown bird with a red breast, trapped in a pretty cage. I can almost feel its wings fluttering within my cupped hands, see it soar upwards towards the sky, towards freedom. A linnet, a finch.

'A beautiful name,' I agree.

34

I have lots of answers now, but not all of them. Were my dreams really memories, hauntings, echoes of the past? Or just the workings of an active imagination trying to make sense of a sad story? I will never know for sure. I'm still not sure that I believe in ghosts, but I am open to persuasion.

The obsession is fading fast. The dresses are only vintage velvet, the gramophone a cool antique, the violin an instrument of torture in Coco's hands. I make sure the door of the powder-blue birdcage is always open now, but still, it's just a pretty place to keep a house plant.

One thing Clara has left me with is courage, honesty, the knowledge that you cannot go along with things you know are wrong. You have to follow your heart, be true to yourself, as she did.

I cannot quite work out where Finch fitted in. The boy in my dreams looked nothing like Sam Cooper, Clara's love. Maybe he was just my imagination's version of a cool gypsy boy? It was a fantasy, a perfect romance conjured up by a girl who wasn't quite ready for a real-life boyfriend. What could be more out of reach than an imaginary boy, one I dreamt up myself from scratch?

The dreams have stopped, and now there is an ache inside me where thoughts of Finch used to be. But you cannot actually miss a boy who never existed to begin with, so I keep this to myself.

I may not be directly descended from the Romany gypsies, but Clara was my great-great-aunt and that means that Linnet was a kind of very distant cousin. Maybe Mrs Lee is right and I do have a sensitivity to shadows and feelings and stories from long ago? I am not about to admit that, of course, because I do not want her to start training me up to be some kind of gypsy fortune-teller with a crystal ball and a spotted handkerchief tied round my head.

It is bad enough telling her that her grandma, Jane Cooper, was a rich man's daughter, a girl who ran away with the gypsies on the eve of her wedding, back in 1926.

❖❖❖❖❖❖❖❖❖❖❖❖❖❖❖❖❖❖❖❖

That her horrified parents were so ashamed that they faked a drowning and let everyone believe she was dead.

Mrs Lee is a permanent fixture in our kitchen these days. She calls in after work a couple of times a week, sipping tea with Mum and passing on the contact details for Linnet's younger brothers and sisters, who are still alive and well and living all around the UK and beyond. Suddenly we have discovered a whole branch of family we never knew we had.

Mrs Lee has been talking to Grace, the museum lady, and the two of them are planning an exhibition in the Kitnor Museum about the local gypsies in general and Clara's story in particular. Mrs Lee is lending her photographs and we are handing over the velvet dresses and the letters and the old engagement ring, as well as the jazz records and the gramophone, the powder-blue birdcage and the violin.

'Keep the violin for as long as you like,' Mum tells Grace. 'Seriously.'

The local paper gets hold of the story and runs a human-interest feature, which is pretty cool, and Mr Wolfe gives us a whole history lesson about it. He asks me to stand up in front of the class in the green velvet dress and cloche hat

❀ ❀

and tell some of the story myself, and although it is scary to begin with, once I get past the first few stumbled sentences, it's actually quite a buzz. Maybe the spotlight isn't such a scary place to be, after all? Millie and Alfie say it is the best history lesson since the time I mummified the Barbie doll.

I get used to the fact that Summer is going out with Aaron Jones and Millie gets used to the fact that Alfie Anderson runs a mile whenever she appears. She is philosophical. 'I've been kissed, anyhow,' she says, with a faraway look in her eyes. 'I mean, BOY have I been kissed!'

Alfie is still pining for Summer, and I have told him politely and honestly that there is no hope whatsoever for him, but he just shrugs and goes on dreaming, and I cannot blame him for that. I am still pining for a boy who never existed, after all.

Alfie and I find that hot chocolate and marshmallows can ease the heartache, though, just a little.

And just when I think the weirdness is through with me, there is one last twist in the story.

We come home from school one day to find Mum and Paddy sitting at the kitchen table chatting to a very cool woman with grey hair cut into a choppy bob. A younger man and woman, with keen, smiley expressions are there too, making notes as they talk and eating marshmallow cupcakes that make the kitchen smell like heaven.

'Oh, girls,' Mum says. 'This is Nikki and Phil and Jayde from the TV company I mentioned a while ago. They're researching locations for a TV film, remember? They are definitely going to use the gypsy caravan in their film, isn't that great?'

'Brilliant!' Summer says.

'We're hoping we'll be able to find the right locations for filming in and around Kitnor too,' Nikki says. 'The country-side has just the right feel to it. We'll film some test shots and then, if all goes well . . .'

'We may just be having a film shot in Kitnor, over the summer holidays,' Paddy says. 'Wouldn't that be amazing?'

A little fizz of excitement begins to bubble inside me.

'With the gypsy caravan?' I check. 'What kind of a film is it?'

'It's historical,' Nikki explains. 'Based on the Romany travellers who lived here years ago. Your mum was show-ing us a feature in the local paper about the girl who lived here . . . Clara, was it? Great stuff. I have a good feeling about all this, and the B&B would make a perfect base.'

I have a good feeling about it too. It's as if the last shreds of winter's sadness have fallen away, leaving me stronger, braver, no longer a shadow girl. The future doesn't seem so scary these days.

I take Fred's lead from the hook by the door.

'I'll take the dog for a run,' I say. 'I'll be back in time for tea.'

Fred runs ahead of me down across the garden, past the caravan where I sat with Alfie on Christmas Eve, down to the woods. The little trees are unfurling soft green leaves and butter-coloured primroses carpet the ground, and there isn't even one marshmallow-soft cloud in the clear blue sky.

I don't dream about the woods any more, of course, or about woodfires or piebald horses or bow-top wagons glimpsed throughout the trees, but wouldn't it be cool if those things were real again, if the film crew based themselves here and re-created the things I dreamt about?

If dreams of the past turned into glimpses of the future?

It could happen.

✿✿✿✿✿✿✿✿✿✿✿✿✿✿✿✿✿✿✿✿

Fred is barking suddenly, yapping and wagging his tail and galloping back to me for reassurance, and looking up I see a figure through the trees, a boy with dark wavy hair and an easy grin, a boy who can melt my insides the way Paddy melts chocolate. My heart is thumping.

It's not real, of course. It can't be.

The boy walking towards me is wearing a red T-shirt and an old army jacket and skinny jeans, and his Converse are muddy and his skin is paler than the way I remember it from my dreams.

'Hey,' he says.

'Hey.'

It's not real, I know, even though Fred is licking his hand and sniffing at his Converse, even though the boy is looking at me with dark blue eyes that make my heart flip over.

'Are you one of the sisters?' he asks. 'The Chocolate Box Girls?'

'I'm Skye,' I say.

'OK . . . hello, Skye! Cool name!' he says. 'Mum showed me the article in that magazine. It's what made her decide to check the place out, because of the gypsy caravan and all. She thought it would be perfect for the film, so here we are.

277

And it's better than she thought, seriously, with the woods and the beach and the village with all those cool old cottages.'

I blink. 'You're here with Nikki?' I manage to say. 'With the film people?'

'That's right – Nikki's my mum,' the boy says. 'If we end up filming here in the summer, I guess we'll be seeing quite a bit of each other. So . . . pleased to meet you, Skye.'

He holds out his hand to shake mine, old-fashioned and polite, and when our fingers touch a crackle of electricity passes between us.

'My name's Jamie,' he says softly. 'Jamie Finch . . .'

Now you know Skye it's time to enjoy her twin sister's story.

Read on for a sneak preview of
the next gorgeous book in
the
chocolate box girls
series . . .

SUMMER'S DREAM

Have you ever wanted something so badly that it hurts? I guess we all have, but I am not lusting after a new dress or a kitten or a baby-pink laptop – I wish. No, my dream is bigger than that, and tantalizingly out of reach.

It's not even an unusual dream – loads of little girls probably share the exact same one. Anybody who ever went to dance class or dressed up in fairy wings and skipped about the living room probably hopes that one day they'll be up on stage with the audience throwing red roses at their feet. For me, the dream stuck; it hasn't been replaced by a passion for ponies, for pop stars, for boys. Even though I have a boyfriend these days, the dream hasn't wavered one bit.

I want to be a dancer, a ballerina, to dance the part of

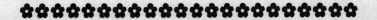

Giselle or Coppélia or Juliet, to dress up as the swan princess in a white tutu made of feathers, to make the audience gasp and cheer. I want to dance, and you know what? It didn't seem like such a crazy idea, back when I was nine or ten.

I push open the door of the Exmoor Dance Studios and go inside, my ballet bag swinging. It's early, an hour before my class is due to start, but the small upstairs studio the seniors use is empty at this time and Miss Elise has always told me I am welcome to use it whenever I like.

I do like, quite a lot, these days.

The foyer is busy with little girls in pink leotards, laughing, talking, buying juice and biscuits as a treat between school and dance class or queuing with their mums to book up for the summer holiday sessions. I used to be just like them, once.

I was good. I got distinctions in every exam I took, danced centre stage at every dance school show, got used to Miss Elise telling the class, 'No, no, girls, pay attention – look at Summer! Why can't you all dance like that?'

My twin sister, Skye, used to roll her eyes and stick her

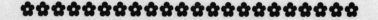

tongue out at me, and the minute Miss Elise's back was turned the whole class would fall about giggling.

Don't get me wrong, though – dance was one thing I always took seriously, even if Skye didn't. I loved it. I signed up for every class the dance school offered: tap, modern, jazz, street . . . but ballet was my first love, always. At home I devoured ballet books about girls who overcame the odds to make their dreams come true. My poster girl was Angelina Ballerina, and I watched my DVD of *Billy Elliot* so many times I wore it out. When I wasn't reading about dance or watching DVDs or dreaming about it, I was practising because even then I knew that being good was not enough; I had to be the best.

Dad called me his little ballerina, and I loved that. When you have lots of sisters – clever, talented sisters – you have to try a little harder than most to be noticed. I guess I'm a bit of a perfectionist.

Miss Elise told Mum she thought I was good enough to audition for the Royal Ballet School, that she would set up the auditions for when I was eleven. I was so excited I thought I might explode. I could see a whole future stretching before me, a future of pointe shoes and leotards

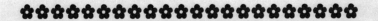

and aching muscles, a future that could end with me in a feathered tutu on the stage at the Royal Opera House.

It was so close I could almost reach out and touch it.

And then everything fell apart. Dad left us and moved up to London and it was like our whole family crumbled. For months Mum looked hopeless and crushed, and there were rows about visits with Dad, rows about maintenance payments, rows about everything. My big sister Honey raged and blamed Mum for what had happened.

'I bet Dad thinks she doesn't love him any more,' Honey told us. 'They've been arguing loads. Dad can't help it if he has to be away a lot – he's a businessman! Mum nags too much – she's driven him away!'

I wasn't sure about that, though. It seemed to me that Dad had been spending less time with us and more time in London for a while now. Mum didn't so much nag as mention quietly that it'd be great if he could be around for Coco's birthday or Easter Sunday or even Father's Day, and that would trigger a big scrap, with Dad shouting and slamming doors and Mum in tears.

When I asked Dad why he was leaving, he said that he still loved us, very much, but things hadn't been perfect for a while

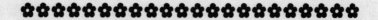

now. Back then it didn't seem like a good enough reason to me. When things aren't perfect, you need to work at them until they are, right? Dad obviously had different ideas.

A few days after the split, Skye, my twin, announced that she didn't want to go to ballet class any more, that she'd only really gone along with it because I wanted to go. That kind of pulled the rug out from under my feet. I always thought that Skye and I knew everything there was to know about each other . . . and it turned out I was wrong. Skye had a whole bunch of ideas that I didn't know about.

'Summer, I don't want to tag along in your shadow any more,' she said, and if she'd slapped my face, I couldn't have been more hurt. It felt like she was cutting loose, leaving me stranded, at exactly the moment I needed her most.

If you'd taken my life and shaken it up and thrown the smashed-up pieces down in a temper, you couldn't have made more of a mess. So . . . yeah, that whole ballet school idea. It was never going to take off after Dad left, I could see that.

I passed the regional auditions OK, but by the time the date rolled around for the London one my head was a muddle of worries and fears. Could I really leave Mum, so soon after the break-up? Could I leave my sisters? I was torn.

Dad had agreed to take me to the audition, being based in London himself, but he was late collecting me and by the time we finally arrived I was sick with nerves. I danced badly, and when the panel asked me why I thought I should be given a place at the Royal Ballet School, I couldn't think of a single reason.

'Never mind,' Dad said, exasperated, driving me home. 'It's no big deal. Ballet is just a hobby really, isn't it?'

That just about killed me. Ballet was a big deal to me – it was everything. I stopped being Dad's 'little ballerina' that day. I'd lost his respect – I was just one daughter of several after that, the one whose hobby was dance.

Needless to say, I wasn't offered a place.

'Don't blame yourself,' Mum told me. 'You've been under a lot of pressure, and I should never have trusted your dad to get you there on time. There'll be other chances.'

I smiled, but we both knew that I'd messed up a once-in-a-lifetime opportunity.

You'd never have made it anyway, a sad, sour voice whispered inside my head. *You were kidding yourself.*

I brushed the voice aside, although I couldn't quite forget it. Sure enough, that voice has been around ever since, chipping

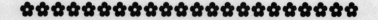

into my thoughts with a bitter put-down whenever I least expect it.

That was over two years ago. Now, I am thirteen and I still love to dance. I still get distinctions in my exams and I still get good roles in the shows. Things at home are better. Dad lives in Australia now, but it's not like we saw much of him anyway, even before the move. Mum has a new boyfriend, Paddy, who is kind and funny and easy to like. They are getting married in just a few days' time. Paddy has a daughter, Cherry, so I have a new stepsister too, and I like her lots.

My big sister Honey can still be a nightmare, especially since Paddy and Cherry moved in, but I have Skye and Coco, a boyfriend, and good friends I can rely on. I do well at school. I should be happy, I know . . . but I'm not. Even though I messed up my chance of dancing professionally, I still have that dream.

In the deserted changing room beside the senior studio, I peel off my school uniform and fold it neatly, wriggling into tights and leotard. It's like peeling away the layers of the real world. In my dance clothes I feel light, clean, free.

I loosen my hair from its long plaits, brush away the day's hassles and braid it again tightly, pinning it up around my head. I have done this so many times I don't even need a mirror any more. I sit down on the wooden bench and pull the pointe shoes out of my bag. I slip my feet into the pink satin shoes and tie the ribbons firmly, tucking the ends out of sight the way Miss Elise has taught me. I stand and walk across the changing room, into the empty studio, the mirrors glinting. Beside the door, I dip the toes of my shoes into the chalky dust of the rosin box, so that I do not slip or slide on the hardwood floor. I reach down and flick on the CD player and the music unfurls around me, seeping under my skin.

When I dance, my troubles fall away. It doesn't matter that Dad left and that my family are still putting the pieces back together again. It doesn't even matter that I never got to go to the Royal Ballet School.

I take a deep breath and run forward, rising up en pointe, curving my arms upwards, swooping, twirling, losing myself in the music. When I dance, the world disappears, and everything is finally perfect.

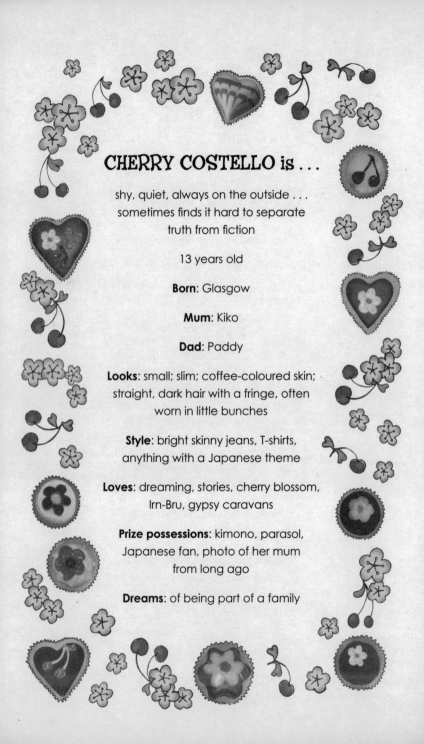

CHERRY COSTELLO is . . .

shy, quiet, always on the outside . . .
sometimes finds it hard to separate
truth from fiction

13 years old

Born: Glasgow

Mum: Kiko

Dad: Paddy

Looks: small; slim; coffee-coloured skin;
straight, dark hair with a fringe, often
worn in little bunches

Style: bright skinny jeans, T-shirts,
anything with a Japanese theme

Loves: dreaming, stories, cherry blossom,
Irn-Bru, gypsy caravans

Prize possessions: kimono, parasol,
Japanese fan, photo of her mum
from long ago

Dreams: of being part of a family

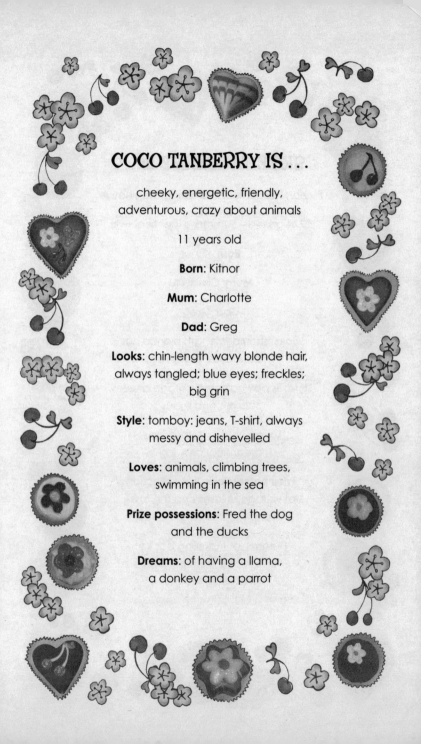

COCO TANBERRY IS...

cheeky, energetic, friendly,
adventurous, crazy about animals

11 years old

Born: Kitnor

Mum: Charlotte

Dad: Greg

Looks: chin-length wavy blonde hair,
always tangled; blue eyes; freckles;
big grin

Style: tomboy: jeans, T-shirt, always
messy and dishevelled

Loves: animals, climbing trees,
swimming in the sea

Prize possessions: Fred the dog
and the ducks

Dreams: of having a llama,
a donkey and a parrot

SKYE TANBERRY is . . .

friendly, eccentric, individual, imaginative

12 years old – Summer's identical twin

Born: Kitnor

Mum: Charlotte

Dad: Greg

Looks: shoulder-length blonde hair,
blue eyes, big grin

Style: floppy hats and vintage dresses,
scarves and shoes

Loves: history, horoscopes,
dreaming, drawing

Prize possessions: her collection
of vintage dresses and the fossil
she once found on the beach

Dreams: of travelling back in
time to see what the past
was really like . . .

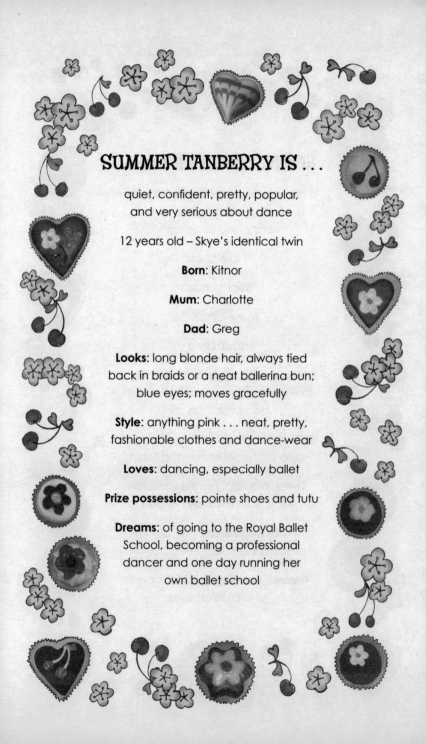

SUMMER TANBERRY IS . . .

quiet, confident, pretty, popular,
and very serious about dance

12 years old – Skye's identical twin

Born: Kitnor

Mum: Charlotte

Dad: Greg

Looks: long blonde hair, always tied
back in braids or a neat ballerina bun;
blue eyes; moves gracefully

Style: anything pink . . . neat, pretty,
fashionable clothes and dance-wear

Loves: dancing, especially ballet

Prize possessions: pointe shoes and tutu

Dreams: of going to the Royal Ballet
School, becoming a professional
dancer and one day running her
own ballet school

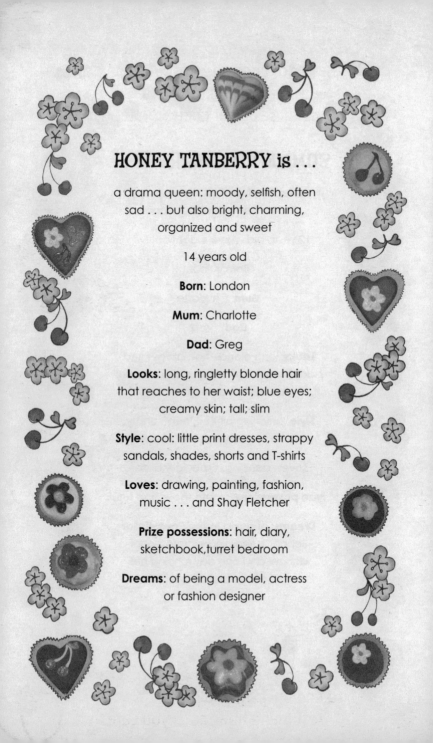

HONEY TANBERRY is . . .

a drama queen: moody, selfish, often
sad . . . but also bright, charming,
organized and sweet

14 years old

Born: London

Mum: Charlotte

Dad: Greg

Looks: long, ringletty blonde hair
that reaches to her waist; blue eyes;
creamy skin; tall; slim

Style: cool: little print dresses, strappy
sandals, shades, shorts and T-shirts

Loves: drawing, painting, fashion,
music . . . and Shay Fletcher

Prize possessions: hair, diary,
sketchbook, turret bedroom

Dreams: of being a model, actress
or fashion designer

Best Friends are there for you in the good times and the bad. They can keep a secret and understand the healing power of chocolate.

Best Friends make you laugh and make you happy. They are there when things go wrong, and never expect any thanks.

Best Friends are forever,

Best Friends Rock!

Cathy Cassidy's
MY
BEST FRIEND
Rocks!
Enter at:
www.cathycassidy.com
mizz
AWARD

Is your *Best Friend* one in a million?

Go to *www.cathycassidy.com* to find out how you can show your best friend how much you care

Cathy's Gorgeous Cherry and Chocolate Cake with Chocolate Sauce

YOU WILL NEED:

2 ramekins
75g dark chocolate, melted – plus extra for serving
50g unsalted butter, melted
2 whole free-range eggs, beaten
50g caster sugar
50g plain flour
50g pitted cherries from a can, chopped
2 tbsp juice from a can of cherries
Butter, for greasing

Place the chocolate, butter, eggs and sugar into a bowl and mix.

Add the flour, cherries and cherry juice and mix together until smooth.

Grease the ramekins with butter, then spoon the mixture into each until they're three-quarters full.

Cover each ramekin with clingfilm, place in the microwave and cook on full power for 4 minutes, or until risen and cooked through.

To serve, turn the puddings out on to plates and drizzle the melted chocolate on top.

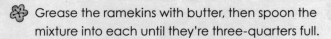
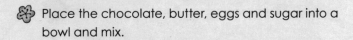

Cathy Cassidy's

Rocking Rocky Road Recipe
– with Marshmallows!

You will need:
2 medium-sized bars of milk chocolate
A couple of handfuls of mini marshmallows
6 digestive biscuits (broken into largish chunks)
A handful of raisins (optional)

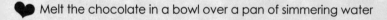

Melt the chocolate in a bowl over a pan of simmering water

Once the chocolate has melted, leave it to cool slightly then add the rest of the ingredients and mix well (but make sure that you don't break up the biscuits too much)

Pour the mix into a baking tray, which has been lined with baking parchment, level out and put in the fridge for a few hours

Once the mix has set, tip it out of the tin and cut into squares, make yourself a cup of hot chocolate and enjoy!

Follow your *Dreams* with all of

Cathy Cassidy's

Gorgeous Books!